The Fairy Lair

A Magic Place
Book Three

by Anne C. LeMieux

ALADDIN PAPERBACKS

Dedicated with love to
Aunt Nancy, Aunt Pat, Aunt Anne,
Aunt Mary, and Aunt Jean

First Aladdin Paperbacks edition October 1998

Copyright © 1998 by ACL Limited, A Connecticut Limited Partnership

Aladdin Paperbacks
An imprint of Simon & Schuster Children's Publishing Division
1230 Avenue of the Americas
New York, NY 10020

Designed by Tova Reznicek
The text for this book was set in Sabon.
Printed and bound in the United States of America
10 9 8 7 6 5 4 3 2 1

Library of Congress Cataloging-in-Publication Data
LeMieux, A. C. (Anne Connelly)
The Fairy Lair : a magic place / by Anne LeMieux. — 1st Aladdin Paperbacks ed.
p.   cm.
Sequel to: The Fairy Lair, a hidden place.
Summary: The faeries call on Sylvia and Dana to help them save their wooded
realm, a place where magic breaks through into the everyday world, when a
real estate tycoon threatens to turn it into a private luxury community.
ISBN 0-689-81727-4 (pbk.)
[1. Fairies—Fiction. 2. Magic—Fiction. 3. Environmental protection—Fiction.]
I. Title.
PZ7.L537375Fah   1998
[Fic]—dc21   98-29378
CIP   AC

The Fairy Lair

A Magic Place

~ Chapter One ~

Sylvia Widden felt it through the soles of her shoes, through her feet, felt it running up through her the way she imagined sap rose in trees—that feeling that spring was on the verge of bursting out of hibernation.

"Coming up?" Dana Brennan's voice floated down from overhead.

Pushing a stray lock of blond hair out of her eyes, Sylvia peered up at the bare branches of the towering oak tree, the Oldest Oak. She could see Dana's head sticking out over the side of the woven branch platform secured in the high limbs of the tree, her private hide-away. The rickety ladder that her friend had made from fallen branches leaned against the huge trunk.

"Not right now," Sylvia called up. She was feeling too restless to sit still up in the tree. She looked around the clearing in the Wildbrook Woods, beyond their neighborhood, the special place where she and Dana had become friends. The sight of the twig-and-stick broom she'd made last summer poking out from under a low cluster of waxy-leafed rhododendron sparked an impulse for spring cleaning. Snatching it up, she jogged over to the Ring of Rocks, a circle of large stones with a huge boulder in the center.

Using the stick end of her broom, she lifted a clump of dead, wet leaves out of the cleft in the boulder. Now she could see the clear water bubbling up from underground, then trickling in a tiny stream down to join the Wildbrook River, which ran along the bottom of the woods, separating the wild of the woods from her street, Wildbrook Commons Lane.

The stream was clogged in spots, too, so she whisked the debris out to the edge of the clearing, all the while keeping her eyes open for a hint of the magic fairy world that this place, more than any other place, seemed to open a window to. F-a-e-r-y, she reminded herself, not f-a-i-r-y, when you were talking about the real thing.

"Have you been up here without me?" Dana called, sounding puzzled.

"No," Sylvia yelled, sweeping her way back toward the Oldest Oak. Little jade-colored curls of ferns and the earliest spring flowers were beginning to poke up out of the ground, and she was careful not to disturb them. "Not since last fall. Why?"

"Well, somebody has." While Dana started climbing down, Sylvia worked her way in a wide circle around the base of the trunk, with rhythmic sweeps. In between two large roots, long and twisted with bumps in the middle like elbows, the twigs of the broom suddenly jumped off the ground, almost pulling the branch handle out of Sylvia's hands. She took a step back, staring at the ground. No burrow holes, no animals, no anything except rich brown dirt. Cautiously, she moved the broom back between the roots. This time she could feel a strong quiver course through the branch, pulsing, the energy running right up into her hands and arms. When she moved the broom away from the spot, the sensation subsided at once.

"That's weird," she said.

"What?" Dana jumped off the ladder, holding what looked like one of her black-covered blank books.

"I felt something when I was sweeping. Here, try it." Sylvia held the broom out to Dana, who took it with one hand and passed it over the roots. She paused over the same spot that had tugged at Sylvia.

"Hmmm. Maybe the aquifer's closer to the surface

here," Dana said. "It's like the broom's acting as a divining rod. That's how they used to find sources of water in the old days, so they'd know where to dig for wells."

"But it didn't react to water when I was over near the spring." Sylvia took the broom back, repeated her actions, and again felt the leap of—something—when she came to the same spot.

"I don't know what it is," Dana said. "But we know this is a magic place. It shouldn't come as any big shock when strange things happen. Like this." She opened the book.

Sylvia looked at the page, which was covered with small sketches of an oak tree, with a leaf and an acorn, drawn in Dana's impeccable and detailed style. The bottom of the page was labeled in runes, the symbols that formed the magical alphabet, with a long, foreign-sounding name in italics, and the common name: *Quercus pedunculata*. Oak.

She looked up questioningly at Dana. "You drew these, right?"

Dana nodded.

"So, what's strange about it?"

"I didn't write the names in. Someone else did." Dana flipped through to another page, where she'd drawn clumps of broad, bright green leaves.

"'*Symplocarpus foetidus*,'" Sylvia read out loud. "What a fancy name for skunk cabbage!"

"I know it's stinky stuff, but it actually is useful." Dana smiled. "Grannie's old herbal manual says the roots can be used to make a medicine for asthma or headaches."

"I think the smell would be enough to *give* someone a headache," Sylvia said. "So do you think maybe Mr. MacCooney's been back? Do you think he labeled your drawings?" Sylvia's former next-door neighbor had been revealed to be more than an eccentric old man who always dressed in blue and liked to hike in the woods. He had a long list of titles, one of which was Oak Master of the Ancient Order of Foresters.

"I don't know. I haven't seen him, but that doesn't mean he's not around." Dana shrugged. "Well, it's getting late, and I still have homework to do. I guess I'd better be getting home."

"Me, too." Sylvia tucked the broom back under the rhododendrons, and the two made their way down the path to the stone bridge that used to cross the Wildbrook River but now was so flood-damaged that fallen pieces of it served as stepping-stones instead.

The river was running higher than usual as snow from last week's late snowstorm melted. Along the banks, a few thin patches of dry-looking white crystals still clung to the ground here and there, but with the first official day of spring not far off, they'd be shrinking away. Bright green cones of skunk cabbage were beginning to sprout. Sylvia and Dana stepped around them. The pungent odor of the wild weed that grew wherever the ground stayed damp was detectable even in these newly grown plants.

"It smells like Janey's desk did when she left half an egg salad sandwich in it over winter vacation," Sylvia said. "*Symplocarpus foetidus.*" She liked the sound of the words. "*Symplocarpus foetidus,*" she repeated, rolling the syllables off her tongue.

Dana's hazel eyes were laughing. "I know. But that's how it protects itself." Then she drew in a sharp breath, staring at one of the clumps. "Look!"

As Sylvia watched, the outer leaf of the plant grew transparent, and a darker green shadow appeared behind it. It looked, she thought, like the cocoon of a monarch butterfly just before hatching. Without breaking the leaf, the shadow burst through and a small green ball rolled across the mud. About the size of a crab apple and as clear as the green glass fisherman's ball that Dana's grandmother had hung in the window of the Brennans' kitchen, it did three somersaults, slowly rolling to a stop. Then small green arms and legs appeared, and a head popped out of the top, like a startled turtle.

Sylvia did a double take. "Skunk cabbage faeries?"

Dana laughed out loud. "Why not? All the flowers have theirs. I've never seen these before, though."

The round green face of the tiny being wore a mischievous grin, as if delighted at having escaped somehow.

"*Symplocarpus foetidus,*" Sylvia repeated again. "Do you think the words are magic?"

"Maybe it's a combination—of magic in the words, and naming. Remember I told you that to name something is to call it? You called them out!" Now she stared seriously at Sylvia. "And maybe it's part you, too—think about what happened up in the Fairy Lair just now. Do you think you're developing magical powers?"

Powers? The idea made Sylvia nervous somehow. "I hope not," she said. "I wouldn't know what to do with them."

Now the little green skunk cabbage faery waddled over to one of the other shoots and walked through it, disappearing for a moment, then reappearing on the other side, pulling a second round green ball with it. After a few somersaults it, too, sprouted limbs and a face, and the two spent a moment running at each other, bouncing off each other's round bellies, falling back, then opening their little mouths in silent, uproarious laughter. Then the two dove into two more cabbages and brought out two more faeries. Those four did the same thing, and four more appeared. The whole troop began rolling, bouncing, and tumbling energetically around the riverbank.

"Aren't they funny?" Dana said, grinning.

Funny as they were, they still smelled like skunk cabbage. Sylvia had to restrain herself from holding her nose, because she didn't want to offend them. But she watched their antics with delight as they rolled at and bounced off each other, and off the small cabbage shoots.

"It looks like a sloppy game of soccer, except there are no players—only balls," Sylvia said, giggling.

"Or like a faery pinball game," Dana said, laughing. "Ouch!"

Two of them had just bumped heads and jumped up, their tiny arms flailing away at each other in a little battle, but too short to reach because of their stomachs.

"What are you guys laughing at?"

A voice as unpleasant as a frog with laryngitis broke in. Across the river stood Janey Toth. At the sound of Janey's voice, Sylvia sensed the ripple of displeasure that ran through the green faery group.

"Oh, no," Dana muttered. "Don't come over."

Although Janey couldn't have heard Dana over the babbling of the brook, she immediately began making her way across the stepping-stone path to the far bank, as if she couldn't be anything but contrary and annoying.

"I have a secret," Janey was saying. "Want to know what it is?"

Sylvia shook her head. "If you tell us, it won't be a secret," she called over.

"No one with a mouth as big as hers could possibly keep any kind of secret," Dana said in a low voice. "She's going to inflict it on us whether we want to hear it or not."

Janey was on the middle stone now, and Sylvia had to stop herself from actively wishing that Janey would slip and fall in the water.

"So, we're moving to a new house—a great big one! It's not even built yet," Janey said, breathing heavily as she struggled to keep her balance. But she kept coming. The round green clowns were growing increasingly agitated as she got closer and closer. Janey didn't appear even to notice them, which didn't surprise Sylvia at all. Most people had no clue about the ethereal beings she and Dana saw. On the second to last stone, Janey's shoe slipped off the mossy edge, sending a wave of water splashing over the cluster of skunk cabbage faeries, who bounced angrily like boiling water in protest.

"Stupid rock," Janey said loudly. She took one long step, her foot landing smack on top of two of the new skunk cabbage shoots, smashing them into the moist dirt.

Immediately a shrill cry of anguish trilled from the green faeries as two of them flattened like paper, then disintegrated into streaks of bruise-colored air and dissipated in the breeze.

"Look what you did!" Sylvia cried out.

Janey was oblivious to the damage she'd just done. "So what? It's skunk cabbage. What's your problem, Sylvia?"

The remaining six faeries had edged back away from their dwellings, and Sylvia could feel the fear they were emanating.

Dana's eyes were glowering with anger. She leaned down toward the tiny green troop and whispered fiercely:

"Symplocarpus foetidus
This one is not one of us.
Use your scent, now, to protect
And teach her how to show respect."

Her words mobilized the skunk cabbage faeries, who began to swell like inflating balloons and float rapidly toward Janey, joining together and enveloping her in a green-tinged, most odiferous cloud.

"Pew! It stinks here!" Janey took a step backwards, stumbling into the water. The protective cloud stayed with her, and she began to cough and sneeze.

"That's funny," Dana said innocently. "It didn't before you came over and smashed the plants. Did it, Sylvia?"

Sylvia shook her head as Janey splashed back across the river, fanning the air frantically with her fingers. She scrambled up the other bank and took off wailing down the street. The green cloud floated back across the river, splitting into small cirruslike streaks that went back into their host plants.

"Do you think they'll come back out again?" Sylvia asked.

"I don't know. But let's not call them back. They've probably had enough of the material world today. Here, hold this." Dana handed Sylvia her book of plant drawings, knelt down, and tried to replant the remains of the two ruined skunk cabbages. But they'd been uprooted, and the roots were torn and flattened. She sighed. "I'll bring these back to Grannie. She can dry them and keep them with her medicine herbs. At least their lives won't have been wasted."

While Dana had been fiddling with the plants, Sylvia had been leafing through the pages, scanning her friend's artwork. Now she stopped at a page near the end, blank, except for some writing that looked like it was penned in the same hand as the labels.

As Dana stood with the skunk cabbage roots, Sylvia held out the open book and pointed. Dana read softly.

> "'*Foresters of the Ancient Order*
> *Enemies are at our border.*
> *If they win, and Wildbrook claim,*
> *Little will be left to name.*
> *T. T. R. MacCooney*'"

"True Thomas Rhymer MacCooney," Sylvia said. Her former next-door neighbor. "Well, at least we know who wrote in your book now."

Dana looked down the river, then gazed at the woods. "Enemies?" she said somberly. "This doesn't sound good."

~ Chapter Two ~

A loud, mechanical grumble from somewhere outside roused Sylvia from sleep the next morning before her alarm clock went off. The grumble subsided, some high-pitched beeps sounded, then the grumble started up again, louder this time and more purposeful. Untangling herself from her covers, she crawled over to her window to investigate.

At the end of the street, in front of the remains of the old stone bridge, bright yellow bulldozers and backhoes were maneuvering around each other in a ponderous, clumsy dance. Sylvia watched as one rumbled slowly over to the edge of the riverbank just in front of the house next door, Mr. MacCooney's house, though he hadn't lived there in nearly a year. Bustling around were half a dozen men, all wearing bright red hard hats. At the direction of one who waved his arms and shouted in gruff tones, the big, jagged-toothed scooper jerked down and came up filled with a chunk of riverbank, which it deposited in a mound near the sidewalk.

"What . . . ?" Before she could formulate the thought, a huge flatbed truck carrying what looked like long steel girders rolled up Wildbrook Commons Lane. The air brakes screeched to a halt in front of Dana's house, right across the street from Mr. MacCooney's.

Quickly Sylvia threw on jeans and a shirt for school and scampered downstairs. In the kitchen, her mother was sipping coffee from a mug, "hatching" into the morning as she always called it, before the rush to get the five Widden children off to school.

"You're up bright and early this morning," Mrs. Widden said in surprise. "Breakfast isn't ready yet."

"That's okay, I'm not hungry yet. The trucks and machines woke me up. I want to go see what they're doing." Sylvia slipped her jacket off the hook by the back door and over her arms.

"Dylan's already out there." Mrs. Widden smiled. "Just don't get too close."

"I won't," Sylvia called over her shoulder as she went through the back door.

Her younger brother, Dylan, greeted her excitedly as

Sylvia came up beside him on the sidewalk. "They're building a brand-new bridge!"

Up close, Sylvia could see several more construction workers with big rubber boots standing down in the river, pounding away with sledgehammers at what was left of the old stone bridge. Her heart sank. The Wildbrook Woods and the Fairy Lair had enjoyed a lot more privacy after a flash flood had washed away the bridge that connected it to the neighborhood.

Now Dana came shooting out her front door. As she ran to the corner of her yard, looking down into the river, Sylvia crossed the street to join her.

"Do you see what they're doing?" Dana asked.

"Dylan said they're building a new bridge."

"That's obvious," Dana snapped. "Look what they're doing to the riverbanks. They've ripped them to shreds."

Sylvia followed Dana over to the edge. It was true. On both sides of the bridge, deep gashes had torn the banks of the river and the fledgling grass and new colony of skunk cabbage. The uprooted plants were squashed in the growing mounds of dirt.

"Oh . . . ," Sylvia said softly in dismay, thinking of the comical little cabbage faeries of the day before and what had happened when Janey ruined two of their skunk cabbage homes. "Do you think they've gone—"

"Back into the Ether," Dana said gruffly.

The Ether was the half-energy–half-material plane from where the nature faeries drew their life. Water, Air, Earth, and Fire—Sylvia named them in her head. And each element had its corresponding elemental faeries— the Undines, the Sylphs, the Gnomes, and the Salamanders, though she'd never seen the last. Plants had their own combination faeries, too—hybrids, Dana called them, because plants are composed of more than one element.

"Their energy went back, anyway," Dana was saying. "Without their host plant existing in the material world, they can't exist."

Sylvia sighed sadly. But Dana was scowling even more angrily. "Who do you think is building this? And why?" Dana's eyes narrowed suspiciously.

Before Sylvia had a chance to respond, Mrs. Widden's voice called from the front door. "Dylan, Sylvia, time for breakfast. Come back inside, now."

"Go ahead," Dana said. "Eat fast, though. We can talk on the way to school."

"Well, I think it's a shame," Mrs. Widden was saying as Sylvia and Dylan squeezed through the back door together. Her mood was clearly no longer cheerful.

Blueberry pancakes steamed from a platter in the middle of the table. "Michael, only three apiece, please," she added as Sylvia's older brother hefted the serving spatula and prepared to dig into the stack.

"And don't hog all the syrup, either," Kathryn said. "There's never enough left after *you* get through with it."

"You don't need sweet stuff," Michael told his older sister. "Sweet stuff gives you zits. Look: I think there's one coming out on your nose already—" He started to point, but Kathryn swatted his hand away.

"Well, it was inevitable, I guess," Sylvia's father replied as he lined up glasses and filled them with orange juice from the pitcher. "The kids have been lucky to have had it for as long as they have."

Sylvia's ears perked up.

"John, that's one of the reasons we bought this house in the first place," Mrs. Widden was saying over the chatter. "And it's not only a place for the kids to play. It's also one of the most beautiful views in town."

"Well, I haven't seen the drawings yet, but I hear the plans for Wildbrook Ridge are very attractive," Mr. Widden said. "Margaret Maven is certainly pumping enough money into the project. I'm told she plans to live there herself."

"Pass the butter, please," Dylan said.

"This is the breakfast table, not the Super Bowl, Michael," Mrs. Widden said sharply as Michael picked up the butter dish like a football. "It's not only a question of money." She looked back at her husband. "Doesn't that Maven woman have enough? She's one of the richest people in the state. Why can't she go build her fancy development somewhere else and just leave the woods alone?"

Fancy houses? Wildbrook Ridge? Was that why they were building a bridge? Sylvia's stomach clenched like a fist.

"Janey said the Toths are going to buy one of the biggest houses up there," Sylvia's little sister Annie informed them. "And there's going to be a private country club with a pool and a golf course—"

"Yes, I heard that about the golf course," Mr. Widden said, his eyes lighting up a little. "It would be nice to have one so close."

"*Private*, John," Mrs. Widden said. Sylvia hadn't heard her sound so upset in a long time. "Only for the few people who have enough money to buy a huge fancy house, which certainly wouldn't be us. Or most of the other people in town. It's such a beautiful piece of land. Why can't she just leave it alone for people to enjoy?"

"Well, technically, it *is* private property," Mr. Widden said. "So in a way, it's been fairly generous of her to allow people access. . . . " His voice trailed off at a look from Sylvia's mother that indicated she wasn't buying his argument. Sylvia could see he was beginning to be very uncomfortable with being on the opposite side of this issue from his wife.

"What's going to happen, Dad?" Sylvia asked now. "Is it definite? That they're going to build houses and all that stuff in the woods?"

Mr. Widden let out a long, slow sigh. "Well, it's all been approved by the Town Planning and Zoning Commission," he said. "And my firm's been engaged as accountants. Now that they've started building the new bridge, it looks like they may be ready to move forward."

"Then why don't you speak to Ms. Maven?" Mrs. Widden said. "Ask her to reconsider."

"Honey, I have a family to support," he said helplessly. "It's a huge account, and I'm not in a position to rock the boat or cause any trouble."

Sylvia's mother pressed her lips together firmly, not saying anything else for the moment.

Sylvia felt almost numb herself. The Wildbrook Woods were *her* woods, no matter what Maven lady owned the property. Since she'd been old enough to leave the yard, they'd seemed like a little country. And ever since she and Dana had discovered the Fairy Lair, the magic place where *real* magic crossed into this world, she'd had glimpses into the hidden elemental world called the Wildbrook Domain. If the faery habitat were destroyed, would the domain be gone forever? And the faeries, too?

Mr. Widden sighed and looked at his watch. "Well, I think we'd better table this discussion for another time, or everyone's going to be late. Kathryn, are you ready to go?" Their father dropped her off at high school every morning on his way to work.

"Almost." She jumped up and rushed into the bathroom, where Sylvia could see her anxiously checking her nose in the mirror. Sylvia stayed at the table waiting for the exit rush to calm down a little and digesting the disastrous news. Feeling her mother's hand on her shoulder, she looked up. A prickle of tears stung Sylvia's eyes. Her mother gave her a squeeze.

"Well, they haven't started chopping trees down yet. I'm going to look into this further. You'd better get going now." Her mother handed Sylvia her backpack and gave her a quick peck on the cheek.

Outside, Dana was waiting impatiently. "We're

going to have to run if we want to make it before the bell."

As they jogged down the block, way behind all the other kids, Sylvia filled Dana in.

"Enemies at the border," Dana said grimly. "We have to go up there as soon as we can, right after school. We have to make a plan."

"What kind of plan?" Sylvia had asked.

"I have no idea. But something."

"Hey, you girls better move back," one of the workmen called from across the river as Dana and Sylvia stood on the sidewalk in front of Dana's house that afternoon. "These machines are dangerous. And don't get any ideas about playing in the woods. They're off-limits, now."

"It's a free country," Dana retorted.

The man scowled at her. "Yeah? Well it may be a free country, but this is private property." He jammed the shovel he was wielding into the ground, propped his foot up on it, and glared at them.

"Come on," Sylvia whispered. "We'll pretend we're backing off, then sneak around the other side of my house and go way back behind Mr. MacCooney's garage, where the river turns."

The two girls started to stroll away, and the man, satisfied, went back to work. Beyond the slight bend where the river meandered, they were out of sight of the workers. They crossed quietly, trying to keep low as they made their way to the special place.

"Whew! We made it." Sylvia went toward the Ring of Rocks to rest a minute. The forest immediately around them was silent. But still, they could hear the faint sounds of the work going on at the river's edge.

"Watch out—" Dana grabbed Sylvia's arm.

Sylvia stopped in her tracks. "What?"

"Salamanders," Dana said. "Don't squash them." She pointed to a decaying, moss-covered log that Sylvia had been about to step on.

"Lizards? Aaahh." Sylvia gave a little squeal, circled the log, and hopped up onto one of the rocks.

"Don't be such a baby," Dana scoffed. "And they're not lizards. Lizards are reptiles. Salamanders are amphibians."

"I'm not a baby, I just don't like creepy-crawly things," Sylvia retorted.

Perhaps three dozen tiny, reddish-orange, lizardlike creatures had scurried out from beneath the log. They darted this way and that over the soft blades of new grass.

But Dana wasn't listening to her protest. "Look—

look at what they're doing. That's weird."

From her perch, Sylvia looked. Suddenly, as if called to order by some invisible leader, the salamanders began to arrange themselves into two lines. Very slowly, they moved forward, toward the Ring of Rocks.

"They look like they're marching in a parade," Dana said. "I've never seen salamanders do that."

Sylvia watched, fascinated. "I didn't know there were any salamanders this far up in the woods. I've never seen them here before, have you?"

Dana shook her head. "I think they usually live in wetlands and marshes. They need a moist habitat— maybe the spring makes it damp enough. But wherever they live, I don't think they act like that." Dana pointed again.

The salamanders had marched between two of the rocks, and were diving, still in a most orderly fashion, into the tiny spring-fed pond. But the surface of the water remained curiously undisturbed, flat and silver-brown, like a tarnished mirror. At first the creatures skimmed it in a small circle.

"There aren't any ripples," Sylvia said. "How can that be?"

Even as she asked the question, the likely answer came to her. When things in the natural world began to act in strange ways, it was usually a sign that magic was about to break through into the everyday world again.

"Because they aren't ordinary old swamp-variety salamanders," Dana said excitedly. "They're Fire elementals."

As the girls watched, a startling transformation began to take place. The tiny lizard limbs stretched out into arms and legs. The pointy heads rounded out, and faces emerged with delicate features, and black eyes sparkling like wet nuggets of coal. Then the Salamanders rose upright. The skin on their backs split like cocoons, and two wings, like a torn cape, spread out. At the same time, little plumes of reddish-orange flame rose from their heads.

Now the Salamanders sank just beneath the water's surface, their formation changing into a more complex pattern. Some swam in a circle. Others made a diamond shape inside the circle. Still others divided the diamond into four triangles. One, larger than the rest, stayed in the very center, twirling, making its own smaller circle.

"It's the City of Light design," Sylvia said. "Just like we saw the other times—the pattern in Mr. MacCooney's garden, and the watermark on the pages of *The Ethereal Blue Book*—"

"Shhhhhh—keep watching."

The bodies of the tiny fire faeries began to glow, as if their skin had turned suddenly phosphorescent. The glow grew golder and brighter until it was almost fiery, and their movements grew so quick they blurred, outlining the pattern in the water. Water vapor began to rise above the wet, flaming design, and the pattern actually hung in the air. Slowly it floated up, going higher and higher over their heads.

Above the opening in the forest canopy, the sky was a pale, mild blue. Now a single cloud sailed into view over their heads. Sylvia and Dana watched as an opening appeared in the middle of the cloud, and the vapor design swept up through it, then was swallowed as the cloud closed around it.

"It looked like they were sending some kind of a message," Sylvia said, turning to Dana. "Like a smoke signal."

"Maybe they were," Dana replied. The two girls leaned back over the water, just in time to see the glowing pattern of the Salamanders' strange water dance fade to a shimmer and wink out. Sylvia blinked. The water was clear. And uninhabited by so much as a water bug. Where had the elementals gone?

*   *   *

"A message from the Salamanders?" Grannie Brennan clucked her tongue and looked very serious. "Of all the elementals, the Fire ones are the shyest. For them to come out in the open to contact the Sylphs, something important must be happening in the Ether."

Sylvia was sitting with Dana at the table in the Brennans' kitchen. A wonderful scent of raisins and cinnamon was wafting from the oven.

"I bet it has to do with the Wildbrook Ridge plan," Dana said.

"That could very well be," Dana's grandmother said. She dried her hands on a woven dish towel with a pattern of fish along the border and glanced out the window. Hanging in front of it was the green glass ball she'd asked Dana's fisherman father to bring home from one of his fishing nets. A protection against anything bad hurting the home, she'd called it. Sylvia watched as Grannie stared at the glass globe, frowning. Formerly clear, now the glass was cloudy, almost as if it had patches of mold on it.

Grannie took it from its hanger and polished it with the towel, then held it up to the light streaming in through the window. It was still cloudy. Slowly, she hung it back up again. "The protection's been weakened." She shook her head. "Time for candles, I said to myself while you two were out."

"Candles?" Sylvia said.

"I wonder if the Salamanders coming out was what gave me the feeling that it was time for me to be making candles again. Our supplies aren't low, but the urge was very strong. Dana, you and Sylvia can take a trip to the marsh and pick me some candlemakers' rush. Let's see if we can lure the Salamanders back and find out exactly what's going on."

~ Chapter Three ~

Wildbrook Commons Lane was uncommonly quiet Saturday morning.

"Thank goodness the construction's stopped, at least for the weekend." Mrs. Widden looked up from the newspaper she was reading. "If they make that much noise just rebuilding the bridge, I don't know how I'm going to stand it when they actually start building dozens of houses."

A percussive smattering of clatters and booms from the basement punctuated Sylvia's mother's sentence, topped off by a resounding cymbal clang.

Mrs. Widden winced, then closed her eyes tightly for a second. "Whatever possessed me to say Dylan could take up the drums?" she murmured. She went over to the door to the basement, opened it, and called down. "Dylan, new drum practice rule: You can only play when the noise *outside* is louder than the noise *inside!*" Now she picked up the newspaper and removed one of the sections. Rummaging in the junk drawer, she brought out a pair of Annie's safety scissors and began to cut out a square.

"What's that?" Sylvia asked. "Coupons?"

Mrs. Widden shook her head. "There are some letters to the editor about the Wildbrook Ridge proposal. One of them has an address for the group that started to protest last year when the plans were in front of the Town Planning and Zoning board. Their petition wasn't enough to stop it from being approved. But they're still trying to get attention. I thought I might contact them. If it's not too late."

"*Too late* . . ." The words echoed in Sylvia's mind, imparting a new sense of urgency.

"Mom, is it okay if I go over to the Brennans'? Dana's grandmother said she's going to make candles today."

"Make candles? What a nice, old-fashioned idea. I sometimes think we'd all be better off if we went back to candlepower instead of all this modern so-called progress." She smiled nostalgically, then nodded at Sylvia. "Go make candles."

As Sylvia made a move toward the door, Michael

came bounding into the room with a wad of sweaty, smelly clothes. "Mom, can you wash my basketball uniform? We have a game tonight." He dropped the uniform on the floor next to the basement door, then exited the kitchen.

Kathryn was close on his heels, a bundle of laundry in her arms, too. "Can you do this first, Mother?" She held up a green and yellow dress. "This has to be washed in cold water and not go in the dryer, or it'll shrink. I need it for the dance tonight. The other stuff can go in the warm–cold cycle, then tumble on medium heat. But wait until after I wash my hair so there's enough hot water for me, okay?"

Mrs. Widden looked wryly at Sylvia. "Then again, there are some modern conveniences I'm not sure I could raise five children without. Like an electric washer and dryer." She sighed. "Candlepower . . . a nice idea, in theory. . . . " She gazed for a moment as if she were looking back in time, then gave her head a quick shake, zipping back to the present. "Kathryn, you're old enough to do your own laundry. You go put it in the washer, and I'll take it out and hang it up for you when the cycle's done."

Sylvia caught her sister's pout as she flounced down the stairs to the laundry in a huff. Giving her mother a sympathetic wave, she left as Mrs. Widden went back to scanning the newspaper columns carefully.

Outside, a low, overcast blanket of gray clouds hung heavily over the still and silent machines parked at the end of the street. The scaffolding for the new bridge was already erected. Sylvia couldn't believe how quickly it had gone up. It was twice as wide as the old bridge and, as far as she was concerned, totally ruined the cozy look the cul-de-sac had always had before.

"I'm ready," Dana said as Sylvia came up the Brennans' back steps. "Let's go."

"Where are we going exactly?" Sylvia asked as they circled around the building site. "At least we don't have to hide from cranky construction workers today."

"About a quarter of a mile past Mr. MacCooney's house, on the same side, there's a marsh where the river splits. That's where the candlemakers' rush grows. It's a little early in the season, and it probably won't be very tall, but we should be able to get enough to make some small candles."

As the two trooped along the bank past Mr. MacCooney's, Sylvia gave a little shiver. The flash flood last summer when the drought ended had damaged the property, and Mr. MacCooney had never repaired the house or moved back in. Formerly a place where the everyday world intersected with the faery world on a daily basis, it now seemed doubly empty and abandoned.

"Where do you suppose Mr. MacCooney is living these days?" Sylvia asked.

"I don't know," Dana said, working her way carefully around a place where the bank was seriously eroded. "He probably spends some of his time in the Ether. Maybe he travels. I wish he'd leave a forwarding address so we could get in touch with him."

Hanging on to a thin maple sapling, Sylvia swung around the precariously caving-in part of the bank. "My mother said there's a group that's opposed to the development. They had a letter to the editor in today's paper. Maybe they'll be able to do something."

Dana shook her head. "I doubt it. Last year when they got up a petition saying there would be too much of a negative impact on the environment, Margaret Maven had all these ecological specialists come in and do studies. They made recommendations, and she had all the plans changed to fit them and then Zoning approved it. I looked it all up in the library."

Ahead of them, the riverbank flattened out, and Sylvia could see roots and lower trunks of slim trees, covered in dark, slowly moving water. Clumps of dried grasses and sedges thrust up from the mirrorlike surface.

"Do we have to go in there to get the rush?" she asked. "I didn't wear my boots."

"I don't think so. There should be some around the edges." Dana rounded a gnarled old sassafras trunk and Sylvia followed, her shoes sinking a little in the spongy ground around the wetland.

"Here's some." Dana squatted down next to a tuft of sharp, green, knee-high grass. She pinched off half a dozen of the stalks at the bottom and, straightening up, gently squeezed the rounded blades. "These should do. I'll check one."

As Sylvia watched, Dana removed two straight pins from the hem of her jacket sleeve. About two-thirds of the way from the pointy tip of the stalk, she stuck one of the pins through, then the other at a right angle, making an X. With one quick downward zip, the pins tore through the grass, at the same time forcing out a single strand of white pith the width of a candlewick, which dropped to the ground.

Sylvia reached down and picked it up. Cool, moist, and spongy, it broke in half as she bent it. "Oh, I'm sorry."

"That's okay. We have more." Dana took one of the

thin, stringy pieces from her and ran it through her fingers. "This is good. Not too dried out, so it should burn smoothly. We'll bring the others back and pith them right before we dip the candles."

"Should we take a run up to the Special Place and check on things real quick?" Sylvia suggested as they headed back upstream.

"Might as well. There's a good spot to cross." Dana changed directions and made a little jump onto a large flat rock in the middle of a shallow stretch of the river.

As they made their way into the woods, the still-bare branches of the trees quivered a little, with a low moaning sound.

"Let's hurry. The wind's picking up. It's probably going to rain soon," Sylvia said, forging ahead easily without the seasonal thick undergrowth that spring and summer brought to the woods to impede walking. When they were about halfway up the slope of the wooded hillside, Dana's hand clamped on to her arm, stopping her short.

"What—?"

"Shhhh." Dana tugged her behind the trunk of a spindly hemlock tree. "Look."

Peering through the fringed pine branches and the tree

trunks, Sylvia saw bits of bright plaid jackets and wool-capped heads on two figures about twenty yards away. Each person was standing next to what looked like a bright yellow three-legged easel with a metal box on top.

"Those look like camera tripods. I wonder if they're taking pictures before someone starts chopping trees down for the golf course or whatever they're going to do," Sylvia said, anger rising inside her.

"Not cameras," Dana said back. "I think they're surveyors. That means they're getting ready to divide it all up into lots to sell."

"How could the Layshee let them in here?" Sylvia asked. "They're supposed to be the guardians of the forest. Look what a hard time they gave us when they thought human beings were hurting the trees." She thought back to the wild and unfriendly reaction that the leafy-looking tree faeries had inflicted on her last fall.

"Maybe the Layshee are dormant, like their trees are dormant in the winter," Dana suggested after a pause. "Because none of the leaves are out on the trees yet—that's how they communicate, through the leaves."

Sylvia crouched beside her to get a better view under the hemlock limbs. Fat drops of cold rain began to splatter down.

"Let's call it a day," Sylvia heard one of the men shout to the other as he began to fold up his tripod. "Ms. Maven, we're going to call it quits," he hollered loudly up toward the top of the ridge. The patter of raindrops became louder, and Sylvia nestled into the scratchy branches for shelter, though she was already getting soaked.

A moment later, a tall woman with short, dark brown hair, sprinkled with gray, came stalking down toward the surveyors. Dressed in a dark gray overcoat, she stood stiffly straight.

"Do you mean to tell me you can't work with a little rain?" Sylvia heard her demand in a voice that sounded harder than steel.

"Pardon me, ma'am, but this here's turning into a downpour, and I'm afraid we can't work in it, no," the other man said apologetically. "But we'll be back bright and early Monday morning. Will that be all right?"

"I suppose it will have to be," Ms. Maven said with a touch of icy scorn in her tone. "See that it's bright and early. I want to survey the lot that's marked for my own personal building site, lot number thirty-seven."

"Where's that, Ms. Maven?"

The woman pointed toward a spot in the woods all too familiar to Dana and Sylvia. "Up there. In the clearing past those scroungy birch trees. You'll know it by the big oak tree on the far side. I'm most eager to have the road cleared up there as soon as possible so we can move those boulders."

"She's talking about the Ring of Rocks!" Dana whispered.

Without another word, Margaret Maven took off in the direction of the bridge.

"Come on, let's follow her," Sylvia said.

Keeping their distance, they made their way down to the river. They watched in silence as the woman strode confidently across the girders of the new bridge. On the other side, she turned once and surveyed the landscape, gave a nod of satisfaction, then stepped into the backseat of a black limousine that was parked, waiting, right in front of Dana's house.

As the big car purred down the street, Sylvia looked at Dana. Her friend was looking grim.

"We'd better get those candles made right away," she said. " And we'd better start thinking about a way to try to get in touch with Mr. MacCooney. The Ancient Order of Foresters are about to lose one of their forests. The enemies are inside the border now."

~ Chapter Four ~

"Soaked to the bone, both of you! No, no, before you tell me what I can see wants to burst right out of you, go upstairs and get some dry things on. I'll put the kettle on for something to warm you from the inside out, so you don't take a chill." Dana's grandmother took Sylvia's and Dana's jackets and spread them out on the radiator, and pushed the two of them toward the hallway.

"Here, take these, Grannie." Dana held out the stalks of candlemakers' rush. "But I think we have a good idea what brought the Salamanders out."

Five minutes later, the two girls were back in the kitchen sipping steaming tea and recounting what they'd seen and heard, while Mrs. Brennan bustled around the kitchen assembling the candle-making materials. The sweatshirt and jeans Sylvia had borrowed from Dana were too big, so she had to roll up the sleeves and the cuffs twice, but at least she was starting to warm up.

"Even a whole group of grown-ups who wanted to preserve the woods and had petitions couldn't stop Margaret Maven's plan," Dana concluded. "What can we do? And what can any of the elementals or faeries do when they start razing the forest? They'll get evicted right back into the Ether."

"Bring me that block of beeswax, please, Sylvia, and put it in the top of the double boiler," Grannie said. Her face was even more wrinkled than usual, scrunched up in thought.

Sylvia brought the hunk of wax, the luminescent hue of a full moon, over to the stove and set it in the silver saucepan that sat on top of a second silver saucepan filled with boiling water. Slowly the block began to melt into a pool of clear liquid.

Dana was pulling the wick centers out of the rushes with her pins and laying them flat on a wooden board.

"Stir this now." Grannie handed Sylvia a wooden spoon, then slowly walked over and sat down at the table. "The elementals don't always mix with each other, any more than they normally mix with humankind. In fact, they sometimes war with each other just the way we do. But the fact that the

Salamanders were communicating with the Sylphs is a good sign that they may realize the need to come together here."

"The wax is melted," Sylvia said, peering into the saucepan. "Do we pour it into molds or—"

"No, we'll be dipping the wicks, not molding," Grannie said. "But not quite yet. Dana, on the top shelf in the herb and spice cabinet is a little jar with a cork seal. We'll be needing that."

Dana pulled a chair over to one of the cabinets, climbed up, and rummaged on the top shelf, bringing out a tiny green glass flask. "Is this it?"

At her grandmother's nod, Dana hopped down and gave it to her. The instant Grannie popped the seal, a delicately sweet scent, both woody and leafy, filled the room.

Sylvia inhaled deeply. "Mmmm—what is it?"

"It's oil of bay and yarrow," the old woman told her. "A powerful combination, both for clarifying the vision of the inner eye and for protection, and it will color the candles properly for our purposes." She carefully let five drops fall into the melted wax and gave another stir with the wooden spoon. Then she removed the saucepan from the stove and set it on the table. Dana picked up the first of the five wicks and dipped it into the fragrant beeswax.

"Dana, let Sylvia and me do that. You have another task to do." Her grandmother gave her a serious nod.

By the time the five thin yellowish tapers were made and had hardened, the gloomy afternoon was sinking toward an even gloomier evening. Raindrops meandered down the kitchen windowpanes, and outside, the woods across the Wildbrook River were stark, black silhouettes—like the skeletons of trees, Sylvia thought with a shiver.

"Have you come up with a proper incantation, my young journeywoman Bard?" Grannie asked Dana with a smile.

"I hope so," Dana said. She set down a piece of paper with rows of neat runes, the magical alphabet they'd learned from one of Mr. MacCooney's old books. "I thought it would be stronger if I wrote it out in runes."

"What do they mean?" Sylvia asked.

Dana translated the verse out loud.

Her grandmother nodded approvingly. "I think that strikes just the right tone. All right, are we ready now?"

At Dana's and Sylvia's nods, she flicked a long wooden matchstick with her thumbnail, and the tip burst into flame. Leaning toward the center of the table where each candle was set in a hole in a flat stone, arranged so the whole resembled an upreaching hand, she held the match to each of the five waxy wicks. Gold-orange flame tongues leaped to life, flickered for a moment, then settled into a steady, even burning. She nodded at Dana.

In a low but strong voice, Dana began to chant:

"Flame of yarrow, flame of bay,
Burn true and bright on this dark day.
Fire elementals all,
Hear the Friends of Faeries' call.
Be not doused by earthly rain—
From deep within Wildbrook Domain
We summon you, the Salamanders.
To your light, the dark surrenders.
What we need to know, reveal
Tell the truth, Ethereal.
Come forth now and don't delay.
Flame of yarrow, flame of bay."

As Dana spoke the incantation, each flame grew brighter and redder, and stretched up toward the ceiling. Sylvia found herself holding her breath, but the flames, like small burning kites with long tails, seemed so strong that she didn't think even a hurricane wind could have made them flicker. Suddenly, with a loud crackle, the flames jumped together, merging into a sleek, transparent red body with four fiery feet and a diamond-shaped head on top.

Around the Salamander's form, curls of orange fire danced. It swayed above the candles, and Sylvia squinted to shield her eyes from the intense brightness. A series of low *whooshing* tones like a distant bonfire's roar began to sound, and somehow inside her head, though it wasn't in words exactly, Sylvia knew what was being said.

Straits in Wildbrook Woods are dire
Threaten Water, Earth, Air, Fire.
O'er the Faery Lair there looms
The shadow of a certain doom.
If together all will fight
There's a chance to change this plight.
If not, the faeries will be banished
Once the Wildbrook Woods have vanished.
Bring the fire to the water
Joined, we'll slow the forest slaughter.
Hide the woods from men who measure
Keeping safe awhile our treasure.

At that, the flames suddenly went out, the Salamander disappearing with them. Wisps of faintly fragrant smoke trailed up from each wick. Dana immediately jumped up from the table and ran out of the room. She was back a minute later with her notebook and a pen and began to scribble rapidly. "I want to write it down so we don't forget any of it," she said in answer to Sylvia's questioning look.

"'Men who measure,'" Sylvia read over Dana's shoulder. "That must be the surveyors we saw today."

Dana looked up at her. "That makes sense. But how can the Salamanders hide the woods from them? What do you think the rest of it means, Grannie?"

Grannie finished trimming the last candlewick with a pair of sewing scissors. "I'm not sure, but the instructions seem clear: 'Bring the fire to the water.'"

"But how will that—" Dana started to say.

"But why—" Sylvia said at the same time.

Dana's grandmother chuckled. "With faery magic, why's and how's aren't always the questions that lead to the true answers." She rose from her chair and took her woven shawl off a hook by the door. "Dana, you carry the candles. Sylvia, get another match from the box in the drawer." She felt the jackets draped over the radiator. "Your things are nearly dry."

"Can I ask *where* are we going and *what* are we doing?" Dana said, following her grandmother's directions.

"We're going to bring the fire to the water," Grannie said simply, opening the back door and walking outside.

The early evening rain had slowed to a tired drizzle, but the ground was soggy from the earlier downpour. Sylvia's shoes squished into the earth as she followed Dana and her grandmother to the far corner of their backyard. The flowing water of the river gurgled quietly as Dana set the stone candleholder on a flat rock by the river's edge. Sylvia handed Grannie the match, which she'd carefully shielded in her cupped hand on the trek across the yard.

The match spit and flickered, then settled into a small flame. But this time, as Dana's grandmother lit the five candles, the flames didn't redden and stretch into Salamander shapes. Instead, they grew paler and paler.

"Look!" Dana whispered. "The Undines are coming."

In the dim light the candles were throwing out into the grayness, Sylvia began to make out the sleek, clear, nearly human forms of the water elementals, who were gathering in great crowds on the surface of the river, upstream and downstream as far as she could see. At their appearance, the whitish flames began to leap in arcs from the wicks to the water. As they did, they seemed to penetrate the Undines, who glowed whitely from within. Their Ethereal bodies began to turn from clear to translucent, then to opaque, and within moments, they'd all merged to form a foggy bank that hovered just above the water's surface.

"The will-o'-the-wisps," Grannie said softly.

As the candles burned, the fog bank grew taller and thicker, drifting slowly toward the woods and up the slope and engulfing the three where they stood.

"What do we do now?" Sylvia heard Dana ask her grandmother, though she couldn't see either of them anymore.

"We let the tapers burn as they will, and we leave the elementals to do their work for the time being."

Chapter Five

"I'm sorry, ma'am, but we just can't continue surveying until this fog lifts." The man's voice, the same one the girls had heard in the woods on Saturday, pierced through the fog, apologetic but firm.

"I'm tired of the delays on this project," a familiar steely voice snapped back. "The clearing of the woods can't begin until we have the surveys accommodating all those environmental changes we were forced into. The building of the homes for which we have contracts can't begin until the woods are cleared."

Dana tugged Sylvia's arm. "It's Margaret Maven again."

Sylvia adjusted her backpack over her shoulders. From the Widdens' yard, they could hear perfectly, even though they couldn't even see the framework of the new bridge. The fog seemed to amplify the voices coming from the foot of the street. Dana, standing right next to Sylvia, looked like a ghost in the thick, chilly, white air.

"I understand that, Ms. Maven, and we'll be up there doing our jobs just as soon as this fog lifts."

"Plan on working overtime to make up for lost time. And, Mr. Smithers"—Ms. Maven raised her voice as if calling to someone who wasn't right next to her—"I trust that a little bad weather isn't going to prevent you from getting that chain-link perimeter fence up. I'm told there were children up in the woods the other day. There's going to be a lot of heavy machinery over there soon, and they may as well get used to the fact that this tract of land is no longer their private playground. I can't afford the liability. Our insurance won't cover it."

"Yes, Ms. Maven, we'll be starting work on that this morning. We should be able to get the posts along the river in by tomorrow. Whole fence should be up in no time," another man's voice answered.

"A fence!" Dana said angrily. "Who does she think she is?"

"She thinks she's the owner of the property," Sylvia answered. "And, unfortunately, she is."

"Sylvia, where are you?" Annie's voice came through the moist white blanket of the air.

"Right here, near the front walk." Sylvia groped

until she felt her little sister's hand. "We're going to have to feel our way to school. Come on, Dana, we're going to be late if we don't hurry."

"This is so strange," Annie chattered as they made their way down the sidewalk. "It's like walking inside a cloud."

Sylvia was beginning to get used to the odd floaty sensation of setting her feet down without being able to see them as they touched the ground.

"Well, as a delaying tactic, it seems to be doing the trick," Dana said. "I don't know how long it can last, though. 'Safe awhile' was what the Salamander said. We're going to have to come up with a backup plan. It doesn't sound like anything can stop that woman."

The fog hadn't lifted by the time school was out. Sylvia was beginning to notice that the longer it hung around, the sharper her other senses seemed to be getting. All day at school she'd been listening to a distant chorus of dully metallic pings, rhythmic and regular, with some pauses in between. Now, as they walked home with the crowd of neighborhood kids, nearing Wildbrook Commons Lane, it seemed to be getting louder.

"This weather is such a pain," Janey complained, tagging along close at the heels of Sylvia, Annie, and

Dana. "My father says it's holding up construction. I can't wait to get into our new house. My mother says I can have a pool party at the new country club for my birthday. If you be nice to me, I'll invite you."

"Don't do us any favors," Dana muttered. "Here's the stop sign on the corner. Turn." The girls rounded the corner onto their street.

"I wasn't talking to you, Dana Brennan," Janey said. "I was talking to—ooofff! Hey, look where you're going!"

"It's difficult to look where you're going when you can't see the nose in front of your face." The jolly voice of Mr. Kunkel, the mailman, came back with a chuckle.

Janey stomped off down the sidewalk, muttering, "People shouldn't hog the sidewalks. Especially civil servants who are supposed to serve citizens, not get in their way. I hope they'll have a less *clumsy* mailman in the new neighborhood." Her harangue was cut short by a thunk and a yell. "Ouch! Stupid street sign!"

"Now shame on a sign that's supposed to be serving the community jumping out and ambushing a citizen that way." There was laughter in Mr. Kunkel's voice, and Sylvia could picture, though she couldn't see, his enormous waxed handlebar mustache bobbing up and down. She felt relieved that his feelings hadn't been dented by Janey's rudeness. Mr. Kunkel had been delivering the mail for as long as she could remember, and she couldn't imagine a nicer mailman.

"You're doing your route late today, Mr. Kunkel," Annie commented.

"The fog is slowing everything down, and perhaps that's not a bad thing. I think things move too fast in this world sometimes. Well, I'd better be off, now. You might want to check your mailboxes," he suggested.

"Mr. Kunkel, did you have any special letters for us today?" Dana asked.

"Special delivery. Very special, indeed," he said seriously and mysteriously, moving away into the fog.

By the time they reached the end of the street, the pounding sound Sylvia had been listening to all day was close and distinct.

"Fence posts, I'll bet," she said in dismay. "That's what that noise was."

"I'm not going to let a little fence keep me away from our special place," Dana said darkly. "I'll talk to you later." And she was off, across the street Sylvia couldn't see to the other side of.

So strange not to be able to see your house from the sidewalk, Sylvia thought. Getting closer, the dim shadow of it appeared as a rusty tinge behind the woolly white-ness, the mere hint of the bricks showing through, all blurry, no outlines.

"Check the mailbox, quick," Annie said as they made their way toward the front porch.

Tapping each concrete step carefully with her toe as she went up so she wouldn't trip, Sylvia reached the mailbox and put her hand inside. It was empty. "Mom must have taken the mail in already. Come on." Opening the door, she held it for Annie.

Inside, all the living room lights were on, and the fog-shrouded windows seemed to throw the glow back into the room, lending it a spooky luminescence.

"Any mail for me, Mom?" Sylvia called out as she headed toward the kitchen.

"Not today," Mrs. Widden told her. Spread out on the table in front of her mother, Sylvia saw several photocopied reprints of newspaper articles. She scanned a few of the headlines over her mother's shoul-der: ENVIRONMENTAL GROUP OPPOSES MAVEN DEVELOPMENT PLAN. KEEP WILDBROOK WILD—GRASS ROOTS MOVEMENT TO PRESERVE TRACT GROWS. MAVEN DEVELOPMENT PLAN REVAMPED. WILDBROOK RIDGE LUXURY COMMUNITY APPROVED BY ZONING BOARD. She checked the top of the paper for dates—last year.

"Did the group just give up after the plan got approved?" Sylvia asked.

"From what I've read, they did all that could be done, but it wasn't enough. It's such a shame." Mrs. Widden gave her head a shake and pressed her fingers to her eyes for a second. "That noise—all day long. It's pounded me a terrible headache." She sighed.

"Are you sure there's no mail for me?" Sylvia asked now.

"Look for yourself, honey. It's on the counter. A few bills and a few pieces of junk mail."

Junk mail wasn't always junk. Sylvia smiled, remembering the Magic Meadow Wildflower Medley seeds she'd received, addressed to Resident Widden. That was almost a year ago. And it had opened the door to the faery world to Sylvia for the first time.

She pounced on the pile and began sifting through, setting the bills aside and examining each piece of junk mail carefully while Annie crowded against her elbow. An envelope full of bargain coupons from local merchants. A flyer for the grand opening of a new car wash. A glossy, oversized light blue envelope with fluffy white clouds decorating it, like preprinted fancy computer stationary. Odd . . . there was no address on it at all, nothing, in fact, except for one word: FREE. Maybe it was an advertisement for new members to one of those clubs, a special introductory offer of free CDs or books if you promised to buy a certain number of them in the future.

Turning the letter over, Sylvia checked the back. No return address, either. Flipping it over again, she stared at the front. The envelope wasn't blue anymore. It was creamy white with black squiggles in it, like birch bark. Turning it in her hand a third time transformed the pattern on the paper into the mottled pink-and-black pattern of a granite rock!

"Did you find the special delivery Mr. Kunkel said he brought?" Annie asked.

"I think so," Sylvia told her. Nodding her head for Annie to follow, she headed up to their room. Once inside with the door closed, Sylvia showed Annie the envelope, which was now covered with a pale green fern print. "Turn it over," she instructed her little sister.

Annie's eyes opened wide. "It went from leaves to waves. How'd it do that? Is it like those Magic Markers that can change color when you go over them with the special one?"

Sylvia smiled. "Not Magic Markers. Real magic."

"Open it!"

Sylvia slid her finger carefully under the flap and

drew out a one-page letter with a border that matched the envelope, now a lacy etching of insect wings. In the center of the page were lines of runes. At the very bottom were some runes she recognized by now—True Thomas Rhymer MacCooney.

"What's it say?" Annie wrinkled her nose.

"I'll have to translate." Sylvia opened her bottom drawer, where she kept all her most special things: her one other letter from Mr. MacCooney, Dana's letters, the birch bark with the award of the Order of the White Swan Wing, which she and Dana had earned last fall, and the index card with the rune key that she and Dana had copied almost a year ago, the night they'd snuck into Mr. MacCooney's garage.

A   B   C   D   E   F

G   H   I   J   K   L

M   N   O   P   Q   R

S   T   U   V   W   X

Y   Z

"Do you have—"

"Here, paper and pencil." Annie pulled a doodle pad out from under her bed and a silver pencil from the cup on her dresser and handed them to Sylvia. She scribbled away busily for a short while, with Annie sitting on the edge of the bed, impatiently tapping her foot. When she'd finished, she read the whole message over slowly, and handed the piece of paper to Annie.

FREE . . . THE FUTURE
Soon enclosed the land will be . . .
And razed, the forest, tree by tree . . .
   Fuelled by fire of human greed
   By those who take more than they need,
Deaf to any other plea.

   Harken, Friends of Faeries, hear:
   Blinded vision you must clear.
   Tap into the Place of Magic
   Lest for all the end be tragic.

Wildbrook Domain's destiny:
All things Ethereal will flee.
   With each acre felled, will bleed
   All nature's magic, and no seed
Can bring back the wild, the free . . .

Harken, Friends of Faeries, come!
Draw the strength and vision from
Earth and Water, Fire and Air.
You can save the Faery Lair.

I. I. R. MacCooney

"What does it all mean?" Annie asked, after Sylvia silently handed her the translation and she sounded it out.

"Well, it's obvious that the faeries know about the plan for Wildbrook Ridge. And Mr. MacCooney does, too. But I can't imagine what they think we'll be able to do about it," Sylvia said slowly.

Chapter Six

"This is the strangest weather pattern I've ever seen," Mr. Widden said, taking a fat file out of his briefcase Monday evening before dinner. "A completely localized fog. Do you know it was blue skies and clear weather across town at the office?"

He set the file on the kitchen table and opened it, pulling out a shiny blue folder with gold letters embossed on it. WILDBROOK RIDGE LUXURY HOMES AND PLANNED COMMUNITY. Sylvia saw her mother frown as she read it.

"Maybe it's a sign that someone doesn't want this construction to move ahead," Mrs. Widden said. "Maybe the powers that be should reconsider before it's too late." She put the lid on a pot of potatoes a little harder than necessary and gave her husband a reproachful look. He started guiltily shuffling his papers.

Sylvia glanced back and forth between her two parents. Her parents rarely disagreed about anything, but
clearly her mother felt her father was on the enemy side
of this issue. The silence now was punctuated by
Michael dribbling his basketball outside in the fog, and
Dylan clattering away on his drums in the basement.
The *thump thump* of the basketball got louder. Three
more *thumps* up the back steps and inside.

Before he could bounce again, Mrs. Widden snatched
the ball out of the air in front of him. "Not—"

"I know, I know, inside." Agreeably, as if he'd just
now remembered the rule his mother had repeated
probably a hundred times, Michael tossed the ball back
outside. "Hey, what's that?" Sidling up next to Mr.
Widden, Michael turned the folder around to read the
lettering. "Cool. Hey, Dad, think I'll be able to caddy at
the new country club?"

Glancing guiltily at their mother, their father put his
finger to his lips and slipped the folder under a batch of
papers.

There was a long, loud, sloppy drumroll. Sylvia saw
her mother wince as she went over and closed the par-
tially open door to the basement. "That pounding all day
long, and now this. All the practicing he's been doing—
it sounds like he's getting worse!" Her mother pressed

her hands to her forehead. "I know it's important to encourage children's activities, but why couldn't he have taken up something quieter, like the harp, maybe?"

Sylvia giggled, picturing her little brother plucking away at a harp. He'd be a lot more likely to try to use it as a bow and arrow, shooting things off the strings.

"I think it's time we put in a little sound-proofing down there," Mr. Widden said, as if glad for an excuse to change the subject from the Wildbrook Ridge project. "I never thought Dylan would take to the drums the way he has. You have to admit, he's been very . . . persistent."

The drumming stopped abruptly, and everyone gave a start, almost as if the sudden silence were louder than the noise had been.

A few tentative snare drum rattles sounded, then stopped short again. A scrambling clamor ensued, with the sound of sneakered feet pounding up the stairs. But it wasn't Dylan who burst through the door. It was Annie. She slammed it hard behind her and leaned against it, as if holding the door closed to prevent something that might be behind her from escaping. It reminded Sylvia of the way she used to stand at their bedroom door and take a flying leap onto her bed, just in case there was a monster underneath.

"Annie, what on earth is the matter?" Mrs. Widden asked. "And was that *you* playing Dylan's drums? Don't tell me we're going to have two percussionists in the family!"

Annie looked at all three of them, her eyes wide and with a peculiar expression that Sylvia couldn't interpret—not fear, exactly; amazement, maybe? She gulped. "Nothing," she said, answering her mother's question. "And—no—I was just trying them out." Casting a glance at the door behind her, she shot out the back door.

Mr. and Mrs. Widden looked at each other and shrugged in confusion, then went back to their tasks.

On the table, the papers from the file were now spread out, and a colorful brochure caught Sylvia's eye. "Can I see this, Dad?" She touched the corner.

At his absentminded nod, she slid it across the table. On the front page was a watercolor landscape of a rolling hillside above a tame blue brook. A country-kind of road meandered all the way through it. Clustered in groups alongside long stretches of green were tiny detailed paintings of fancy houses. In the middle was a large, elegant-looking complex of buildings. Squinting, she read the teeny-tiny sign: WILDBROOK RIDGE COUNTRY CLUB. On the bottom of the page, in fancy gold lettering, were the words: COME LIVE THE LIFE YOU'VE BEEN DREAMING ABOUT . . .

Opening the brochure, she found herself staring at a photograph of Margaret Maven standing next to a scale model of the project, smiling a stiff smile. In a small box below the photo was a caption quoting the woman: *Wildbrook Woods has been in the Maven family for generations. The time has come to share the beauty, with the building of Wildbrook Ridge Luxury Community.*

Below that was a paragraph telling all about the facilities that residents of the luxury community would enjoy. The opposite page had details of costs and drawings of the different kinds of custom houses that a person could have built, and the address and phone number of Maven Enterprises, with a coupon to send in for additional information.

Let's see—a hundred houses, at . . . Sylvia checked the prices again. Doing the math in her head, she gave a little gasp.

"What's the matter?" her father asked, looking up from his printout of numbers.

"Margaret Maven is going to make millions of dollars!"

Mr. Widden nodded. "To add to her other millions."

Slowly Sylvia closed the brochure and stared at the

front page again. Wildbrook Woods—without any trees. Oh, there were a few neatly landscaped patches between the fairways of the golf course, and here and there in the yards, but . . .

"What a joke—to call it Wildbrook Ridge," she burst out. "It won't be wild anymore." She jumped up, let the brochure drop down to the floor, grabbed her jacket, and ran out the back door.

"I don't blame her for being upset, John," she heard her mother say behind her. "I'm upset, too."

As Sylvia wandered around the side of the house, she could see the fog was finally beginning to thin a little. She could make out the ghostly outline of the new bridge structure, and across the river, all along the bank, tall, dim, gray stripes.

"Is that you, Sylvia?" Dana's words came floating across the street.

"Yep." Sylvia headed toward her voice, and they met in the middle of the street.

"Can you believe how fast they put up those fence posts? And there's a gate on the far side of the bridge with a huge padlock on it." Dana shook her head. "The fog's clearing up, too. I'll bet the workers will be back tomorrow. We're running out of time."

"You should see the plans for Wildbrook Ridge."

Sylvia described the brochure her father had brought home.

"I can't understand how Margaret Maven could have grown up around here and now be ready to destroy the woods." Dana shook her head in disgust.

Sylvia was silent for a moment. "I guess that's not the way she looks at it now. Hey, did you get the special delivery letter, too?"

Dana pulled out of her pocket an envelope similar to the one Sylvia had received. "About the woman being a girl and mustering my power—"

"That's not what mine said. Mine said we had to clear blinded vision and—wait, let me see if I can remember the whole thing." Sylvia slowly recited the rhymed message from Mr. MacCooney.

"It's completely different from mine. Look." Dana took out of the envelope a piece of paper with the rune verses translated and handed it to Sylvia.

In the Ether, years unfurl . . .
Once the woman was a girl . . .
Journey back, the path to trace
To a special time and place.
All your tools and all your power

You must muster at this hour.
Forgotten secrets hold the key
To altering this destiny.

"I don't know what it all means, yet," Dana said. "But it's obvious Mr. MacCooney thinks there's something we can do."

"I just wish I could figure out what it was," Sylvia said. "Once this fog lifts, the construction's going to start again."

"I know," Dana said. "Unless . . . "

"Unless what?"

"Unless we can think of another way to stall it some more. We all have to fight together, the Salamanders said. I wonder . . . "

At Sylvia's questioning look, Dana suddenly grinned. "This battle's not over yet. We need to put together a plan of attack."

The fog had completely burned off by the time they got home from school the next afternoon.

"Look, the fence is up," Annie said in dismay as they approached the end of their street. Across the peacefully flowing river at the foot of the woods, the sunlight was bouncing off a bright silvery wall. It was tall and sturdy looking. The sight made Sylvia's throat tighten. Being fenced out of the woods felt almost like being imprisoned, somehow.

"They can't keep us out. We'll—we'll dig under it. Or something," Dana said, staring grimly at the obstacle.

"What good will that do us?" Sylvia said. "In the end, I mean. It's not going to stop the whole project."

As the three girls stood there watching the construction, Dylan scooted around the back of a bulldozer and hailed the driver. "Hey, can I have a ride?"

"Dylan, you traitor!" Sylvia yelled over to her brother.

He flashed her a grin, but repeated his request. The man in the driver's seat was shaking his head, but smiling. "Sorry, son, no time to play here. We've got a schedule to keep to or the boss'll have our heads."

Just then, the same black limousine they'd seen the other day purred up the street and parked in front of Mr. MacCooney's house. The grumbling and grinding of all the heavy machinery halted. From the back seat, Margaret Maven emerged, carrying a leather portfolio of papers and looking most businesslike. When she saw Dylan talking to the operator of the equipment, she strode over angrily and yanked him back by the shoulder. "Get away from there, young man. What do you think you're doing?" Towering over him, she glared down. "You stay away from here or I'll have a policeman posted. I can't afford a lawsuit if a nosy child gets hurt on my construction site."

Dylan pulled himself out of her grasp, danced away and, to Sylvia's amazement, stuck out his tongue. "My father says you're rich enough to afford anything," he shouted. "So if you're so rich, how come you're so grouchy?"

Sylvia saw the bulldozer driver smother a grin with his hand and try to look innocent as Margaret Maven turned back to him. "And you get back to your job—if you want to keep it." She strode angrily toward the foreman, who flinched visibly as she began to talk to him.

"Good for Dylan," Dana said. "Too bad there aren't any grown-ups willing to stand up to that old crank."

"You said what?" Mr. Widden exclaimed as Annie recounted the story over dinner that night. "You said your father—are you trying to get me fired?"

"It's okay, Dad, I didn't tell her your name," Dylan said reassuringly.

"If I'd seen that woman touch you, I would have gone out and given her a piece of my mind," Mrs. Widden said. She looked at her husband. "Whose side are you on, John?"

"I'm on the side that needs to keep my job and not offend our biggest client," he said. "I know how upset everyone is, but there's nothing we can do about it. The development is going in. And that's the way it is. Dylan, I want you to stay away from the equipment, from the building site, and especially from Margaret Maven, do you understand?" Mr. Widden's voice was stern.

Dylan slumped in his chair, but nodded.

"And, honey, I'd appreciate a little support from you on this," Sylvia's father continued, looking at her mother.

Mrs. Widden pressed her lips together and rose from the table. "I'm afraid I can't support what I don't believe in, John," she said. "And I suppose now is as good a time to tell you as any—there's a protest being organized to picket. I plan to be there."

Sylvia watched her father's jaw drop.

There was silence all around the table. Kathryn was holding her fork halfway to her mouth, just staring at their parents. Michael was nervously buttoning and unbuttoning the top button of his shirt.

"You can't do that!" Mr. Widden sputtered.

"I have to do it," Mrs. Widden said, putting her hands on her hips.

Dylan looked guilty, as if he felt he'd started the

argument between his parents. "May I be excused, please?" Neither parent answered him for a moment.

Finally Mrs. Widden said, "You can be excused to do your homework."

Dylan opened his mouth as if to protest, then seemed to think twice as he eyeballed his parents' expressions, closed it again, and slunk away, grumbling.

~❦ Chapter Seven ❦~

"Sylvia, you have to come down to the basement with me, quick." Annie tugged at Sylvia's arm so hard, her science book slid off her lap onto the floor next to her bed.

Annoyed, Sylvia leaned over and retrieved her homework and looked at her sister. Annie was wearing the same wide-eyed expression she'd worn the day before. "What's going on?"

Annie bit her lip. "There are—well, I don't know what they are—but they're in the basement. Little tiny guys with—I don't know, some kind of tools."

Sylvia raised her eyebrows. "Little tiny guys with tools?" she repeated.

Annie nodded vigorously. "I was playing Dylan's drums again and—"

"If Dylan catches you touching his drums, he'll throw a fit," Sylvia interrupted.

"I was playing real soft. Sylvia, listen to me. They hopped right out of the cracks in the cement wall, where it used to leak. Come see. Quick, before they go away."

Bursting with curiosity, Sylvia set her book down and followed Annie.

Down in the basement, Sylvia looked around. The rough gray walls of the foundation, with darker cracks where her father had patched it here and there, glistened slightly. In the dim light of the overhead bulb, everything looked normal, as far as she could tell. Over near a long table piled with folded clothes, the washer and dryer were both chugging away at loads of laundry. Storage boxes were stacked up along one wall, and old pieces of furniture along the other.

Next to the workbench, piled untidily with tools and remnants left over from household projects, some squares of chicken wire from the fence of the unsuccessful tomato garden her father had attempted one summer leaned in a sloppy tangle. And in the far corner sat Dylan's drum set near two old file cabinets.

"Where are they?" Sylvia asked.

"I don't know. But they were here," Annie said. "I couldn't see them too well yesterday. They stayed huddled in the shadows. But I knew they weren't animals or rats or anything. And I wasn't scared—"

"You sure looked scared when you ran upstairs," Sylvia commented.

"Not scared, not really," Annie said. "But they took me by surprise."

"They came out when you played the drums?" Sylvia asked.

Annie nodded.

"Do you think they're related to the pixies?" Sylvia's sister had met with faery beings before—pixies, the music faeries who'd first made their appearance when Annie was learning to play her recorder last fall.

"I don't think so," Annie said doubtfully. "They didn't have wings or anything." She hunched down, peering along the shadowy sides and in the corners of the basement, then tiptoed over to the drum set.

Cautiously she picked up Dylan's drumsticks and lightly tapped the snare drum a few times. Nothing. She clutched the sticks a little tighter and tapped a little louder, a little more evenly. Suddenly a movement in the darkness near the bottom of the wall behind the drums caught Sylvia's eye.

"Keep going, nice and easy," Sylvia whispered. The shadowy movement spread. As her eyes adjusted, Sylvia began to make out more distinct forms . . . the forms of little tiny guys with sledgehammers, crowbars, and pickaxes so small, they looked like toys! She counted ten of them. No taller than squirrels and with hair and beards as shaggy as squirrel fur, clad in dirt and stone-colored clothes, the tiny guys marched in a circle to the soft, even drumbeat, mumbling what sounded like a work chant in voices surprisingly deep, in a language Sylvia didn't know.

Biting her cheeks to keep from laughing, she watched the one who seemed to be the leader direct his crew over toward the workbench. Moving in a line, still marching, they clambered up the sides of the bench, poking into their surroundings as they went along with their little hands and their tools.

"It's almost like a dance," Annie whispered. "The way they move, I mean. All together like that."

"It's because they're all moving to the same rhythm," Sylvia said. As she said the word, it struck a chord in her memory, something Dana had said when they were in the woods one day when Dana had first told her about the elementals. The Deep Rhythms, which all life is tied into. It was the reason that all the stories of the Ethereal world were told in rhyme, in the old Bardic Tradition. Suddenly, it came to her.

"What are they?" Annie asked.

"They have to be some kind of gnome," Sylvia told her. "The elementals of the Earth."

As soon as she pronounced the word "gnome," all the tiny men halted their activity and looked at her.

"Why are you here?" she asked. "Why have you come?"

"Can they understand you?" Annie asked, still tapping away.

Now the leader spoke, his voice gruff but keeping to the rhythm of the drumbeat. Sylvia felt something inside her head take the strange syllables and turn them into thoughts, into a strong, singsonging language she could understand.

"Gnomes we be
Wild and free
Earth and stone
Bred in the bone
Men have come
Damage done
Holes they dig
Deep and big
Scar the land
Give command
Strike the tone

With iron and stone
Gnomes will fight
Wrong will right
Make them cease
Live in peace."

"Did you hear that?" Annie asked.

Sylvia nodded, keeping her eyes on the head gnome, whose dark eyes glittered like beads of coal. "What can you and the gnomes do?" she asked him.

He tilted his head, frowning in a puzzled way.

"Try rhyming," Annie suggested.

Sylvia searched her brain frantically for the words to try to communicate with the gnome, attempting to put the same rhythm in her voice that he had, hoping he could understand her.

"What can you
Try to do?
How can gnome
Save his home?"

At that, the little fellow's expression cleared, and he turned to his crew, barked some orders, turned back to Sylvia, and laughed a deep, resounding laugh. Instantly, the other gnomes swarmed all over the chicken-wire fence pieces with their tools, attacking them furiously. Within a minute, the fencing was completely unraveled into long strings of thin wire.

A slow smile spread over Sylvia's face. "The fence!" she said to Annie. "We may not be able to stop the construction, but there might be another way to slow things down."

The chief gnome and all the others were standing still now, looking at her expectantly. What had he said? *"Give command/Strike the tone/With iron and stone . . . "*

"I'll be right back," Sylvia said.

"Wait, where are you going?" Annie asked a little nervously.

"You know the horseshoe hanging on our bedroom wall? The one I found in the river the day I found my good luck rock? That's what I need to strike the tone with iron and stone."

"Why?"

"It's a special way to command the gnomes. You keep playing, so they'll stay."

"Okay." Annie continued to tap lightly and evenly on the snare drum.

Sylvia was off like a shot, and back a minute later with the rock and the horseshoe. "We have to hurry," she said breathlessly. "Mom said it's time for us to go up and get ready for bed. She looked suspicious about us being down here, but I didn't give her a chance to ask questions."

On her way upstairs and back, Sylvia'd tried to compose a proper command in her head. She cleared her throat nervously, then gripped the horseshoe and clanged it hard with the good luck rock. Immediately, all the gnomes straightened up and looked at her, as if for orders.

"Now I give you
This command:
Wildbrook gnomes
With tool and hand
Go unweave
The fence of steel
Imprisoning
The Ether-real."

The gnomes began to march in place. Their little leader saluted Sylvia. And she and Annie watched in astonishment as the elemental work crew marched right through the cement foundation, disappearing one by one.

The door at the top of the basement stairs opened, and their mother's voice floated down. "Time to get ready for bed, you two. I hope all your homework is done."

"Coming," Sylvia called out.

Annie set the drumsticks down. "The gnomes have homework, too," she giggled. "Do you think they'll get it all done? That's a lot of fence, and there's only ten of them."

"I have a feeling ten gnomes with magic tools can probably do—or undo—as much as any work crew of Margaret Maven's," Sylvia said.

Though she couldn't see them in the dark, Sylvia could hear from her bed what she thought must be the gnomes at work—a faint metallic tapping, interspersed with a springy whirring sound, like the mechanical music of the works inside an old grandfather clock. As she strained her ears to listen, she felt herself relax as if under a hypnotic spell, not even realizing she'd fallen asleep until the silence when the noise stopped woke her with a start.

The night sky outside her window was a deep but luminous blue. A creamy crescent of moon was framed by the upper-left windowpane. Not a bright enough moon to light up the whole sky like that, she realized, and sat up abruptly. Now she could see the bluish light bathing the night was coming not from the moon, but from Mr. MacCooney's backyard.

There, standing in the middle of the garden behind his house, was her old neighbor! Not in the formal Blue Bard robes he'd been wearing the last time she saw him, but in his old blue plaid bathrobe, the way he used to be. His white hair hung nearly down to his waist, and his fluffy beard was moving as he addressed the gnomes clustered in a tight circle around his feet.

"What's going on?" So intent on watching the scene below the window, Sylvia hadn't even noticed Annie was awake until her sister bounced onto the bed beside her.

"I think Mr. MacCooney might be moving back into his house," Sylvia whispered.

As she spoke, the gnomes broke their formation and went scurrying off in all directions.

"But it's still a wreck," Annie said. "It never got fixed after the flood." She pressed her nose up against the window.

Suddenly Mr. MacCooney turned and looked.

Annie ducked. "Do you think he saw us spying on him?"

Sylvia could see his blue eyes twinkling with an inner light as he waved a hand, and she was so glad to see him again that she forgot to be embarrassed. "It's okay." She waved and smiled, then moved away from the window.

"Now what?" Annie asked.

"Now we go back to sleep and see what the morning brings." Sylvia lay back on her pillow, thinking maybe things might start to improve with Mr. MacCooney back in the neighborhood.

❦ Chapter Eight ❧

"This is impossible!"

A shout, loud enough to be heard from outside, woke Sylvia early, before her alarm rang. A voice she recognized by now—Margaret Maven's.

Throwing off her covers, she scrambled to the foot of her bed and looked out the window. Another sunny day. She clapped her hand over her mouth in astonishment, not at the weather, but at the changes wrought overnight. Mr. MacCooney's house was in better repair than it had been when he'd lived there. The boards that had covered the broken windows were gone, and all the windows had new panes of glass. The door of his garage workshop, which had been hanging by a hinge, was sturdily reattached. And above the door, the old wooden rune sign with the initials for the Ancient Order of Foresters engraved in it was straight once again, flanked on either side by a brightly polished horseshoe.

Not only the buildings were good as new again. The overgrown, neglected yard was neatly landscaped, the white stone paths neat in their circle and diamond design, all the earth newly turned over and ready for planting.

But beyond that, across Mr. MacCooney's yard and the river, the sun wasn't glinting off a long, flat span of chain-link fence. It was shining brightly on what looked like tangled silver tumbleweeds that sat in clumps between the fence posts.

From the street, hidden from view by the brick house next door, the woman's tirade went on. "A chain-link fence cannot simply unravel. Either it was grossly defective, in which case I want a refund from the fence contractor, reimbursement for the labor and for the overtime it will cost to get that fence back up, *or,* and I think this is far more likely, vandalism was involved— in which case I want the perpetrators tracked down and apprehended immediately!"

A slow grin spread across Sylvia's face. The gnomes must have put in some overtime last night! Quickly she got dressed and went downstairs. Both of her parents were peeking outside from behind the living room curtains, with Dylan trying to squeeze between them. And Mrs. Widden was actually giggling. "Well, it looks like someone is on our side!"

She stepped back from the window, and Sylvia's father turned around with a serious look on his face. "Honey, I'm very concerned. If this protest group you've gotten involved with is committing acts of vandalism, you could be in trouble. Destroying property isn't the way to make your feelings known, and taking down the fence could get folks arrested."

"This couldn't have been done by my group," she told him. "We're pursuing strictly legal channels." She peeked around the curtain again. "Look at it—it's been completely dismantled. And to be honest, I can't say I'm sorry. I wonder who did it. . . . Whoever the vandals are, they must be awfully clever with their hands."

"This is none of our business," Mr. Widden said, nervously pulling the curtain closed. "Well, I mean, it's my business, but only the accounting part. We have to stay out of this." But Sylvia's mother was already walking into the kitchen. Slipping back upstairs, Sylvia went into her and Annie's room and tugged at her sister's covers.

"Mmmmph," Annie muttered. She tugged the covers back and rolled over, burying her face in the pillow.

"Annie, come look." Sylvia tugged again. "The fence."

"What about it?" Annie mumbled.

"The little guys with tools did their gnome-work last night! And that Maven lady is out there throwing a fit. I'm going out." As she left the room, she could hear Annie scrambling out of bed.

"Wait for me, I'll be right there," Annie called.

A moment later, Annie came whizzing down the stairs, where Sylvia was waiting at the bottom. "Your shorts are on backwards, and your socks don't match," Sylvia pointed out as they headed out the front door.

"Who cares," Annie said. "Wow!" she said a second later, surveying the damage from a corner of their front lawn.

From where they stood, Sylvia could see an unhappy-looking man cowering in front of Margaret Maven. He was scratching his hard hat as if in confusion and kept looking over at the unraveled fence, frowning, while she barked into a cellular phone.

Moments later, a police car whipped around the corner of Wildbrook Commons Lane and sped down to the foot of the street, pulling up with a screech next to the bridge. Two officers, one old and one young, got out and walked briskly over to Margaret Maven. They pulled out small notepads and began writing quickly as she talked angrily, waving her arms toward the unraveled fence.

The officers looked around, and the older of them caught Sylvia's eye and frowned.

"Uh-oh," she said to Annie. As she took a nervous step back from the sidewalk onto their front lawn, she saw Janey Toth pedaling her bike frantically down the street to find out the scoop on the commotion.

The frowning officer strode toward them, arriving just as Janey did. "Do you children know anything about the vandalism of the fence?" he asked sternly.

Sylvia's thoughts scrambled for an answer that wouldn't be a lie. Did they know anything about it? Well, yes. But she didn't think this policeman would believe an answer that involved tiny magic men with tools. In fact, he might think she was making fun of him.

"We didn't touch the fence, officer," she said, putting as much sincerity as she could in her voice. Annie nodded vigorously in agreement.

"But maybe he did," Janey said, pointing across the bridge.

The officer whirled around. Mr. MacCooney, in his

old blue baseball cap and hiking clothes, was emerging from the woods and coming down the path in their direction. He carried his gnarled old walking stick like a band leader's baton, and Sylvia could just hear the tune he was whistling, the song of the four faery cities and the faery capital, the City of Light.

Quickly the older policeman forgot about the kids and trotted back to join the other officer and Margaret Maven, the three of them standing together as Mr. MacCooney walked spryly across the framework of the new bridge.

"Do you know you're trespassing on private property, sir?" the younger officer said.

"Do you think they're going to arrest Mr. MacCooney?" Annie whispered anxiously.

"Well, if he was trespassing, they should," Janey said smugly. "It's against the law. When the new road goes in, there's going to be a private gate with a guard."

Sylvia tried to ignore Janey. "I don't know," she said to Annie, and strained to hear the conversation that was taking place as the officers questioned their neighbor. "He doesn't look worried, though."

"A campaign of sabotage," Ms. Maven was saying loudly. "What were you doing on my property?" Her gray eyebrows drew into a fierce frown as she stared at

Mr. MacCooney. The old man peered back at her without saying a word out loud, his blue eyes glittering beneath his bushy white eyebrows.

Sylvia was so intent on watching the interview that she didn't notice Dana's arrival on the scene until Dana was standing next to her.

"What's going on?" Dana demanded. "And what happened to the fence? Did Mr. MacCooney do something to it?" She scanned the scene, and a wondering expression came over her face. "When did he get back, anyway? And who fixed his house?"

"Gnomes fixed his house and unfixed the fence," Sylvia told her in a low voice.

"What? What are you talking about?" Janey said shrilly.

"Nothing," Sylvia snapped, signaling to Dana that she'd fill her in on the whole story later.

"Ms. Maven, do you want to press charges for trespassing against Mr."—the younger officer checked his notepad—"MacCooney here? We'll have to investigate further to see if he's involved with the vandalism."

A strange expression was coming over Margaret Maven's face as she looked into Mr. MacCooney's eyes. She stopped talking and slowly closed her mouth, looking uncertain, almost troubled, for the first time since

Sylvia had seen her. She tilted her head and looked up at the woods, staring hard as if trying to see something through the trees. Then she gave her head a small shake.

"Ms. Maven?" the officer repeated.

Now Mr. MacCooney was smiling gently at the woman.

"Ms. Maven, do you want to press charges—"

"No, no, never mind. No charges," she said. "I— never mind." She turned abruptly away from the two policemen and walked to her limousine. The driver got out and opened the back door for her, holding it while she paused to turn around and glance back at Mr. MacCooney with a faraway expression on her face.

"Well, he won't be allowed in the new neighborhood once it's built, anyway," Janey said with a sniff, sounding disappointed that Margaret Maven had somehow let Mr. MacCooney off the hook.

Exchanging a look of mutual disgust, Sylvia and Dana turned their backs on Janey. The officers looked at each other, then at the limo. Everything suddenly seemed to slow down, the moment almost stopping like a freeze-frame in a movie. Mr. MacCooney gave Sylvia a wink, then slipped quickly through a pocket in the air. Then the world sped back up to normal time as the officers looked back to the spot where Mr. MacCooney had been standing beside them a fraction of a second earlier.

The older one's jaw dropped in astonishment. The younger one squinted at the air.

"Where'd he go?" Janey asked, blinking.

"Probably took a shortcut through the Ether," Dana whispered to Sylvia.

"The what-ther?" Janey demanded.

"I wasn't talking to you," Dana said rudely.

The two police officers were shaking their heads at each other. Without another word, they went back to the squad car and drove down the street. With a disdainful sniff at the others, Janey took off after them on her bike.

"All Widdens, in the house now," Mrs. Widden called out from the front door.

"Gotta go. Breakfast," Sylvia said to Dana. "I'll see you in a little while."

Dana, who'd been gazing thoughtfully toward the woods where Margaret Maven had been staring, turned around. "Remember what my special delivery letter said? *Once the woman was a girl.* . . . I wonder if it meant Margaret Maven. And I wonder . . ."

Sylvia raised an eyebrow.

"I have to go eat breakfast, too. I'll talk to you later." Dana ran back across the street, and Sylvia followed her sister inside.

"Why do all those people keep stopping?" Annie asked.

About a block and a half away from their street, as they walked home from school, Sylvia could see a small crowd of people on the corner, some of them holding what looked like picket signs. A few of them waved their signs at the passing traffic on Western Avenue, and some of the cars pulled over. Whenever one did, another person would scurry over and hand the driver a piece of paper through the car window.

"Some kind of demonstration, it looks like," Dana said. "Hey, isn't that your mother?"

As they drew closer, Sylvia gulped in a deep breath of air. One of the scurriers with a stack of papers *was* her mother! Now they were near enough to read the signs:

SAVE WILDBROOK WOODS—
DONATE TO THE PUBLIC PURCHASE FUND

OPEN SPACE
DESERVES A PLACE
IN OUR COMMUNITY

WILDBROOK WOODS—OPEN COUNTRY
NOT COUNTRY CLUB!

"Mom, what are you doing?" Annie cried out, running up to Mrs. Widden.

"I'm being a concerned citizen!" She handed each of the girls a leaflet, calling a special town meeting to try to arrange to block the development of Wildbrook Woods and persuade officials to have a referendum vote for the town to purchase the land for open space. "We don't have much time to try to stop this."

A few of the cars whose drivers accepted leaflets were turning onto the street and driving down to the end to take a look.

"Do you think there's a chance you can?" Sylvia asked.

"I don't know," her mother said quietly. "But I couldn't not try."

A big black car pulled up to the curb next to the demonstrators.

"Uh-oh, here comes trouble," Dana muttered.

Margaret Maven stepped out of the backseat. She

was wearing a dark blue business suit, and her mouth was set in a small smile, but Sylvia thought her eyes looked hard. "May I have your attention for a moment, please," she said in an authoritative, but not mean, voice.

The group of demonstrators stared at her in amazement.

"You got our attention when you brought in the bulldozers," one scraggly-looking younger man called out, but a man next to him shushed him.

Margaret Maven overlooked the heckler's remark. "I would like to extend an invitation to all of you to attend a special meeting at my offices to discuss the Wildbrook Ridge project. Tomorrow night, seven o'clock, at Maven Enterprises, next to city hall. As fellow citizens, I'm sure we can air and resolve our differences and come to a common understanding." She gave a nod.

Nobody said anything. Then, to Sylvia's astonishment, her mother took two long steps over and thrust one of her flyers into the businesswoman's hand. "And *we'd* like to extend an invitation to *you*, to attend our meeting," she said firmly. "I do hope you'll come."

Looking too amazed to speak, Margaret Maven looked down at the flyer, swallowed, then without saying either yes or no, got back into her limousine and drove away.

"Wow, that was brave, Mom!" Annie said, giggling.

Mrs. Widden looked startled, as if she'd only suddenly realized what she'd done. "Why, yes, I . . . I guess it was!"

~ Chapter Nine ~

Sylvia watched across the Brennans' table as Dana carefully finished shading the bark of the Oldest Oak on the landscape she was drawing, a picture of the Fairy Lair. "To remember it by when it's not there anymore," Dana had said glumly when starting it.

"We can't give up." Sylvia had gotten mad and racked her brain to think of some strategy. In the end, she'd had an idea. But now she was having doubts about it. They had to muster all their power, Mr. MacCooney's letter had said. She didn't feel very powerful right now, especially when she looked at all the changes that powerful Margaret Maven, with her money and her machines, had already wrought.

"Do you think we can do it?" she now asked Dana.

"Well, what else can we do? Your mother won't let you sleep over because it's a school night. But we've both traveled through the Ether in dreams before. And we've done it together. I mean, it's not like we'll be a million miles away when we go to sleep. You're only across the street. You sound like you're in the same mood I was in before, ready to give up."

Dana's grandmother, who'd been busy over at the counter setting tiny germinated seeds into brown peat pots to get ready for planting in her garden, spoke up. "Dana tells me that the power has gotten stronger in you, too, Sylvia. Up in the woods, you called the little cabbage faeries, and they came. And look what you accomplished by leading the gnomes. The power to communicate with the elemental world is a gift. There comes a time when a gift must be used."

"Can I see your translation of your letter again?" Sylvia asked Dana.

Dana pushed the letter across the table and began to sharpen a pale jade pencil.

Sylvia reread the words to herself. *In the Ether, years unfurl . . ./Once the woman was a girl . . ./Journey back, the path to trace,/To a special time and place.*

"Think you can draw us a dream-map?" Sylvia said, only half-joking.

"We don't need a map to get to the Special Place. We can use the Oldest Oak as our compass. Just the thought should zip us there." Dana looked down at her drawing and smiled.

"This is more than just dream-travel," Sylvia reminded her. "It's time-travel, too."

Dana fixed her green eyes on Sylvia's now. "Sylvia, you read in your own letter what will happen if we don't do something. It'll all be gone."

"Well, maybe the grown-ups' plan—the meeting and the referendum—will work," Sylvia answered.

"Do you believe that?"

Sylvia sighed. "No, not really." She could see from the look on Dana's face that Dana didn't, either.

"It says go back to the time and place. How do we know when? What time, I mean?"

Dana set her pencil down for a minute and thought. "I guess the only real clue we have is the line *'Once the woman was a girl.'* So if we suspect it's Margaret Maven, we try to picture her as a girl."

"That's impossible." Sylvia shook her head.

Dana laughed. "No, it's not. Just stretch your imagination muscles." She pulled her notebook over, picked up a regular pencil, and closed her eyes for a moment, as if she were trying to see something inside her eyelids. Then she opened them and began sketching rapidly. A minute later, she held up the notebook. On it was a tiny loose sketch of a girl about their age who bore an unmistakable resemblance to Margaret Maven.

"How do you *do* that?" Sylvia shook her head in amazement.

Dana smiled and shrugged. "I don't know exactly." She went back to her other drawing.

For some reason, the prospect of a dream-journey frightened Sylvia this time. The first time, when she'd found herself visiting Gneissus, King of the Gnomes, had been accidental. The second time, when she and Dana had gone together to try to find out the polluting secrets that the Recovco company was hiding, well, they'd been together then. But to venture out in the Ether alone? What if she couldn't find Dana? What if she got lost and couldn't find her way back to her own body? Would that mean she just wouldn't wake up? Just keep on sleeping?

"There is some danger, Sylvia," Grannie said now, addressing Sylvia's fears as if she'd spoken them aloud. "In my dream-travels, I always take a talisman with me, just in case."

Sylvia raised her eyebrows. "A talisman?"

"Yes, a little something imbued with your own personal magic. It acts like a compass. I'm going to give you one. You concentrate on it as you fall asleep, and when you want to return from the dream-world, you focus on it again."

Dana's grandmother went over to one of the drawers and pulled out the half-burned stub of one of the candles they'd made, then came over and handed it to Sylvia. "You helped make this, so part of your energy is already in it. Hold this candle and hold this thought:

> *"Candle, candle*
> *In my hand*
> *Light my way*
> *To light of day.*
> *Candle, candle*
> *I command*
> *Yarrow, bay,*
> *Home, I say."*

Sylvia repeated the verse twice. "That should be easy enough to remember."

Mrs. Brennan nodded.

"There! Done!" Dana held up her picture.

"Dana, it's perfect." Sylvia examined the drawing. The Oldest Oak, in miniature, looked so alive it almost leaped off the paper.

"Take a good look to get your bearings. It's your

map." Dana smiled, then carefully slipped the paper into her big sketch pad.

"I need to get home now." Sylvia stood. "What time do we want to try to meet?"

"How about eleven o'clock?"

Sylvia nodded, clutching the candle.

"Just hold tight to your talisman," Grannie said, patting her shoulder.

"*What* is *this?*" Mr. Widden was holding up the evening paper as Sylvia came into the kitchen.

Mrs. Widden looked at it closely. "It's a picture, dear." She frowned slightly. "I wish I'd known they were taking it. At least I would have smiled."

"I know it's a picture. What I want to know is why you're in it, with this group of—of radicals carrying protest signs! Against my company's largest account!"

"Well, I'm in it because I was there distributing leaflets yesterday afternoon when the newspaper reporter showed up," Mrs. Widden answered with a bright smile.

"That's not what I mean! I mean, why were you there at all?"

Sylvia's mother folded her arms across her chest. "I told you, I'm speaking out for what I believe in. Do you know how little open space is left in this town?"

"Hey, Mom, you're famous!" Michael burst in carrying a second copy of the newspaper. "Front page! Good going."

As Mr. Widden glared at him, Sylvia saw her brother sense the tension between their parents.

"Uh, speaking of going, that's just what I was about to do. See ya." He gave Mrs. Widden a little thumbs-up and sprinted out of the room.

"Wildbrook Woods is not public land, it's private property," Mr. Widden said. "And as private property, subject to the guidelines of zoning law, the owner is free to do whatever he wants to do with the land."

"She," Mrs. Widden corrected.

Mr. Widden threw up his hands, tossing the paper on the table. Sylvia edged over to get a look at it.

"Fine, she," her father repeated. "She, the owner, has to pay substantial property taxes on the land."

"Well, maybe she the owner would get a substantial tax write-off of some kind if she donated the land to the town," Mrs. Widden replied.

Mr. Widden took a deep breath and said in a slightly louder voice, "She, the owner, is entitled in a capitalist society to engage in a profitable business venture. That's what makes this country run! And people need houses, for heaven's sake. Where would we all be if developers didn't build houses?"

Dylan skidded through the room on his way toward the basement. "We could live in tree houses," he said. "Like the Swiss Family Robinson. Wouldn't that be cool?"

"It would be very cool in the winter, especially when it snows!" Mr. Widden said emphatically.

His wife looked at him sympathetically, but Sylvia could see she hadn't changed her mind one bit. "Sometimes there are higher concerns at stake than one person's rights. And in my opinion, this is one of those times. You sound like you've absorbed all the public relations propaganda Margaret Maven is trying to put across. And I'm just not buying it."

"None of us will be buying anything if my boss sees this and decides to fire me!" Sylvia's father groaned and shook his head. Her mother bit her lip, looking worried.

Candle stub warm in her hand, Sylvia rolled over for what seemed like the hundredth time. The little numbers on her alarm clock glowed. Past ten-thirty, and she couldn't get to sleep. She'd tried counting sheep, the flowers on her wallpaper, even just numbers, backwards from a thousand. But though her body was tired, her mind was wound up like a top, thoughts spinning in circles, everything she had to remember. The Oldest Oak, the Special Place, a younger Margaret Maven, her talisman to guide her back . . .

Bringing her fist up to her pillow, she inhaled the faint fragrance of the herbs. The image of the five candles burning on the table, the flames transforming into the Salamander centered itself in the middle of her unsettled thoughts, and had a calming effect. Bay and yarrow, bay and yarrow. The words began a singsonging motion inside her mind, almost rocking her brain with the rhythm. *"Bay and yarrow, once the woman was a girl . . ."*

A slow, faraway tremble started up somewhere below her, started coming toward her, growing in strength. She'd felt that sensation before, she remembered dimly, sleepily. A lifting feeling, inside a rumble like soft thunder, and suddenly Sylvia felt herself rise.

The lightness, the freedom to swim with incredible swiftness through the air, was overwhelming. Hovering for a second in her room, she saw her own shadowy form below her in bed, and Annie in hers.

"Good, you made it. Remember, don't try to talk."

Dana's voice inside her head acted like a magnet, pulling Sylvia out the window, out over their street.

Seeing a glowing oval floating above the silvery ribbon of the river, Sylvia directed her mind toward it and instantly found herself next to Dana.

Dana pointed down. Through the shadowy world of the Ether, Sylvia could make out the old stone bridge.

"Where's the new bridge?" she asked mentally.

"Look closely. This is new, now. Or then," Dana's answer came back.

The night was fading rapidly into dawn, then day. A bright sun rose like a fast-forwarded film, and Sylvia saw it was true. This wasn't the stone bridge she had known, old and weathered even before the flood had damaged it beyond use. This looked like it had just been built.

Slowly whirling in the air, Sylvia looked back down the street and gasped inwardly. The street was a dirt lane. Some of the land was cleared into broad green fields, but much of it was wooded. Wildbrook Commons Lane didn't have nearly so many trees, Sylvia thought. And these were all fully leafed, so whenever they were, it had to be summer. All the brick houses had vanished completely—there was only one house there, a big white wooden farmhouse, with a veranda all the way across the front!

The door opened.

"How can you even *think* about doing this?" a girl's

voice shouted. "Tear down our house so other people can live here?"

"It's already decided, Margaret," a man's stern voice replied. "And I don't think you have any reason to complain. The new home I'm building for our family will be twice as big and twice as nice."

"I don't care *how* big it is. It'll never be home to me." A foot stomped, and a tall girl about thirteen, wearing funny-looking, old-fashioned blue jeans and a white blouse, came storming out, clutching something heavy in her arms. "You didn't have to do this. We don't need the money."

"You come back here, young lady!" The man in a suit came to the door, and he looked almost identical to Margaret Maven, the businesswoman. The girl ignored it and strode angrily to the edge of the yard, with a gait Sylvia recognized immediately. The man stared after her but didn't say anything else.

Dana soared down behind her, and Sylvia followed. Up close, she could see the girl looked very much like the sketch Dana had drawn. And she looked very upset about something, her face tear-stained. Turning in the direction of the stone bridge, she—Margaret—began to walk toward it resolutely.

At the edge of the lane, she bent down, plucked

something from a tuft of weeds, and tucked it in her pocket. When she reached the bridge, she didn't go across it right away but scrambled down the riverbank, splashed her hand in the running water until she found something, put it in her pocket, then ran over the bridge and on up into the woods.

Sylvia and Dana swooped through the trees after her. The sensation was dizzying, but as she practiced steering up and over branches and around tree trunks, Sylvia found her flight more and more controlled. "I feel like an elemental myself. Like an air faery."

She heard Dana's chuckle in response. "You can change your name to Sylphia. I know what you mean, though."

Margaret's path took her directly to the glade. A few times, she glanced over her shoulder with a little frown.

"Do you think she can see us?" Sylvia asked.

"I don't think so," Dana replied. "Not see exactly. But maybe she senses us." Sylvia and Dana followed her through the birch trees in the Fairy Lair, where Margaret walked straight to the Ring of Rocks. She sat on one of the rocks, and now Sylvia could see what she'd been carrying—a gray rock, the size and shape of a large grapefruit, like a miniature of the big boulder

that sat in the center of the Ring. She set it down carefully on the ground, where it fell into two perfectly
matched halves that fit like puzzle pieces.

"A geode!" Dana pointed to the inside of the rock,
each half of which was encrusted with glittering violet
crystals forming two tiny caves.

"Amethyst, it looks like." It was the most beautiful
stone Sylvia had ever seen.

Now Margaret was pulling items out of her pockets
and laying them on the ground beside the geode. A gold-
en dandelion in full bloom. A small dark stone with a
white ring around it, very much like Sylvia's good luck
rock. And a tiny blue glass bottle, which she took and,
stepping over to the trickle of water that flowed from
the underground spring out of the cleft in the boulder,
filled with the clear water, and put the stopper in.

As if following a carefully laid plan, she went back
to the crystal-studded rock, placed the bottle inside the
small cavity of one half, then added the stone and the
dandelion. Finally she fitted the other half of the geode
in place and stood up.

"What do you think she's going to do?" Sylvia won-
dered.

Dana, hovering beside her, shrugged.

Walking slowly over to the foot of the Oldest Oak,

the girl set the round rock down again, this time taking care that the two halves stayed together. Using her hands, she started to dig in the earth between two big roots. When she had a hole twice as deep as the rock, she picked it up and carefully placed it in the ground, then covered it with dirt and packed it down.

"Look!" Dana pointed to a deep blue shadow materializing behind the Oldest Oak. Fuzzy at first around the edges, the vision sharpened as the shadow moved forward toward the girl. Mr. MacCooney!

Sylvia tried to focus harder. He seemed to be the same age as he was now. Or not now—but would be in the future, if they were actually back in the past. Or had Mr. MacCooney stayed the same all the years since Margaret Maven was a girl? Could she see him as they did, then or now or—whenever? Confusion seized Sylvia's thoughts, and the sudden disorientation made her feel like time was spinning around her. Abruptly, she felt herself spinning with it, away from the girl, Dana, the Oldest Oak, from the Fairy Lair.

A wild and dizzy flight was sweeping Sylvia through the Ether like a tumbleweed in a tornado. Images whirled below her—the woods, leafy and full, then flaming with fall colors, the river, the old farmhouse, the brick houses, there for an instant, then gone again, a steep slope of plowed-up dirt and heavy machinery, rising above the river cloudy with sediment, a parade of flaming Salamanders winking out like birthday candles in a hurricane.

Sylvia closed her eyes and clenched her fists, struggling to slow down the turbulent journey, to regain control. A lump in her hand, warm, half-soft—the candle, her talisman. The words to the chant came back.

> *"Candle, candle*
> *In my hand*
> *Light my way*
> *To light of day.*
> *Candle, candle*
> *I command*
> *Yarrow, bay,*
> *Home, I say."*

Immediately, the tornado thickened, and Sylvia felt herself falling down through the funnel, landing at the bottom with a soft thump. Opening first one eye, then the other, she found herself looking up at her bed, sitting on the floor in a twist of covers. Out her window, the dawn was just beginning to rise over the ridge.

❧ Chapter Ten ❧

"I think maybe it happened because you were afraid it was going to happen," Dana said.

"It was scary. I don't think I want to try that again without a guide." Sylvia tossed a pebble in the water and watched the ripples spread in a circle. From the edge of Dana's backyard, they could see the workmen near the bridge. Already new rolls of chain-link fence were being secured to the posts.

"I wish you could have heard what Mr. MacCooney and Margaret said to each other," Sylvia said. So strange to have overlaid her image of the brusque, unfriendly businesswoman with this new picture of her as a girl.

"Well, I didn't because all of a sudden you disappeared. Just blinked right out. I woke up right away. But the trip did give me an idea," Dana said. She stared down the riverbank. "Think we have a chance to sneak up to the Special Place and back before they get the whole fence rebuilt? If we cross upriver a little ways, they won't see us and we can cut across the top of the ridge."

"Maybe. If we hurry. What do you want to do up there? I don't want the police to get called again. My father would go berserk at this point if I got arrested for trespassing."

Dana didn't answer right away. She walked over to the back porch and picked up a wooden stick. She strolled back, balancing it on her finger. "Remember the faery wand I used to get into Mr. MacCooney's workshop the night we first found *The Ethereal Blue Book*?"

Sylvia nodded. It was from the crab apple tree in Dana's backyard, and she'd used it to make a gap in his hedge for them to get through that, too. The way Dana had described it then, it focused a certain kind of natural power.

"And remember the way your twig broom was acting like a divining rod the other day?"

"Ohhhhh." Sylvia's eyes widened. "Do you think the geode might still be there?"

Dana lifted her shoulders. "Let's go see."

* * *

In the woods, the tree branches were just beginning to sprout a delicate green fuzz. Little pockets of the earliest wildflowers had sprung up in the past week, white bloodroot, yellow crocuses, pale purple myrtle. The forest floor felt spongy beneath Sylvia's shoes, the compressed layers of old leaves and pine needles having worked, through the winter, into a dark, rich loam that sent up the smell of fresh mushrooms as they scuffed across it. The *rat-tat-tat* of a woodpecker punctuated the distant sounds of the work crews, the clank of metal, the rumble of the backhoes and bulldozers.

When they reached the glade, Dana and Sylvia crossed to the Oldest Oak in silence, and Dana handed Sylvia the wooden wand. Grasping the thicker end with a light touch, Sylvia slowly began to sweep it across the ground around the roots. Working in a spiral, she circled the tree a few times, trying to remember exactly where she had felt that surge of energy the first time. Suddenly a cool current shot through her wrists, making the hair on her arms stand up.

"Here! I felt something."

Dana dropped to her knees and began brushing aside flaky layers of ground. Sylvia set the stick against the tree and started digging beside her. When they were wrist-deep, Sylvia noticed that small black insects were skittering all over her hands. She shook them off, shuddered, and moved back.

Dana gave her a look.

"I can't help it. I just don't like—"

"I know, creepy-crawly things. It's okay, I'll do it." Dana attacked the ground again for several minutes, enlarging the hole, her arms in the ground past her elbows. "I think I feel something!"

Sylvia leaned over and saw a patch of dark gray, rounded, that Dana's digging had just uncovered. "How did it get way down there? It didn't look like she'd buried it that deep."

Dana stuck her hands back down, carefully loosening the packed soil. "Well, there've been forty years of leaves falling and composting into dirt." Slowly she lifted the stone sphere from the hole in the ground. "I can't wait to see what's inside."

Now Sylvia reached out and touched the rock. "Do you think we should open it?"

Dana stared at her. "Why not?"

"Well, if there's any kind of magic in there, and if it could do any good, maybe keeping it closed will keep the force concentrated. I was thinking—"

"You're right." Dana nodded. "Margaret Maven

should be the one to open it after all these years."

The two girls looked at each other. "The meeting tonight," they said together.

All through dinner, Sylvia watched her mother shoot anxious glances at the clock. Mrs. Widden had said she and Dana could come to the meeting, too, though Sylvia hadn't told her the real reason—she'd told her that they had a lot of facts about trees from an Arbor Day project they were working on in school that might help persuade the businesswoman that saving the woods was important.

"I think it would be good for Margaret Maven to face members of the future generation whom she'll be depriving if she proceeds with this project," had been Mrs. Widden's comment.

At 6:35, Sylvia's mother jumped up and whisked her father's plate off the table before his last forkful was halfway to his lips. Mr. Widden paused, his mouth open.

"All right, everyone," Mrs. Widden was saying briskly as she bustled around the kitchen, covering the leftovers, putting ingredients away. "I'm pressed for time tonight. Kathryn, would you do the dishes, please? Sylvia, you can clear the table since you're coming with me. Michael, you'll have to help Dylan and Annie with their homework, and—"

"What's the rush?" Mr. Widden asked. "Where are you going?"

"I have a meeting that starts at seven o'clock, and I don't want to be late. I'm not sure what time I'll be home, so just make sure the younger ones get their baths and—"

"PTA meeting?" Mr. Widden asked. "Why is Sylvia going?"

"Ummm, no . . . " Now Mrs. Widden began rummaging busily in a drawer, not meeting Mr. Widden's eyes.

"This wouldn't by any chance be connected with the Wildbrook Ridge development, would it?" Mr. Widden sounded increasingly suspicious.

Sylvia's brothers and sisters were looking back and forth between their parents, like watching a Ping-Pong match.

Their mother mumbled something and opened another drawer.

"Ahem!" Mr. Widden cleared his throat loudly. "I said, this wouldn't—"

Mrs. Widden closed the drawer, spun around, and crossed her arms. "I heard what you said, dear. And yes, as a matter of fact, it's a meeting with Margaret Maven, a meeting to which she extended the invitation."

Sylvia held her breath, waiting to see if the situation was going to erupt into a full-blown argument between her parents. The two of them exchanged silent messages with their eyes. Finally, her father spoke. "I guess you have to do what you feel you have to do."

"Yes, I do." Her mother walked over and kissed Mr. Widden on his bald spot. "Thank you for understanding."

Dana's knock at the back door brought an end to the conversation as Sylvia and her mother grabbed their coats and hurried out the door.

"What's that, Dana?" Mrs. Widden asked as she saw the bulky brown-paper-wrapped package Dana was carrying.

"It's a—present for Margaret Maven. Something from the woods." Dana shot Sylvia a raised-eyebrow look. "Did you tell her?" she mouthed.

Sylvia shook her head.

"That's a nice idea," Mrs. Widden said as she backed the car out of the driveway. "Maybe it will help set a friendly tone for the meeting."

* * *

The parking lot of Maven Enterprises was half full when Mrs. Widden pulled in, past the guardhouse, where a uniformed security guard made her sign a list on a clipboard, then copied down her license plate number.

"My goodness, that seems awfully . . . military," Sylvia's mother murmured.

Another guard was stationed outside the main entrance to the three-story brick building.

"We're here for the meeting with Ms. Maven, about the Wildbrook Ridge project," Mrs. Widden told him.

He opened the door for them with a courteous smile. "That's down the hall, and to the right, in the main conference room." Then he saw what Dana was carrying and frowned. "Excuse me, miss, what's in that package?" he asked, his voice no longer sounding so friendly.

"It's just a little gift for Margaret Maven," Dana said. Sylvia saw her gulp. "It's a rock."

"I'll have to ask you to unwrap it and let me see," he said. "There have been some unpleasant threats aimed at Maven Enterprises."

Dana peeled back the brown paper halfway and held it up for him to examine. The guard ran his finger across the surface, looking a little puzzled. "It's a rock," he repeated Dana's words.

She nodded.

"We live on the same street that Margaret Maven grew up on—well, it wasn't a street back then." Sylvia rushed to try to provide an explanation that would satisfy the man. "We found this rock, and we both liked it, and thought maybe it might remind Margaret Maven of when she was a kid and—"

Now the guard smiled. "I see. All right, then." He nodded at Mrs. Widden. "My son has a rock collection. I can't say that I can see Ms. Maven changing her mind, but it's a nice try. Go ahead. And good luck!" He waved them down the hall.

"That was close," Dana murmured to Sylvia as they went down the long hallway. The plush, emerald-colored carpeting swallowed the sound of their footsteps as they followed the guard's directions.

The door to the conference room was open, and as they stepped inside, Sylvia saw about two dozen people gathered in clusters, milling around the large marble conference table. She recognized some of them as the ones who'd been handing out leaflets with her mother. There was quiet chatter and an air of nervousness, as if everyone felt awkward and out of place. On a table against the wall stood a silver urn, next to a tray of fancy cookies and stacks of bone-colored cups and saucers with gold trim. The smell of coffee wafted through the air, but only a few of the guests had poured themselves a cup.

"I don't see Margaret Maven," Mrs. Widden whispered, checking her watch. "It's nearly seven o'clock."

As soon as the words were out of her mouth, a hush fell over the room. The businesswoman, flanked by two men in gray suits, strode into the room, smiling a thin-lipped smile that seemed phony to Sylvia. She nodded at a few people, who moved aside to let her pass, and walked over to the large window on the far wall, which was covered with fancy fabric shades that were closed so no one could see out.

In front of the window, a big easel was set up, with a stack of posters on the ledge, the first one the watercolor map of the planned development. Dana started easing up alongside the table until she was a few feet away. Sylvia followed close behind her, while Mrs. Widden fell in with a group of her fellow protesters.

Margaret Maven faced the silent room. Everyone looked at her expectantly. "My friends," she began.

A sarcastic snort from the scruffy young man who'd made the bulldozer comment the other day interrupted her. "Friends, ha," he said in a loud whisper, but someone else shushed him.

A red flush spread across the woman's face, but she

continued in a firm voice. "I'm here to talk to you about the future."

To Sylvia's astonishment, Dana took a long step forward and held out what was in her hands, letting the brown paper fall to the floor as she did. "And we're here to talk to you about the past," she said.

A fleeting look of annoyance at the second interruption crossed Margaret Maven's face, but then her eyes rested on the geode, and a transformation occurred. Her posture slackened, and she looked unsteady, as if she'd just been knocked over by an unexpectedly large wave at the beach. Her steely gray eyes went wide with amazement, and, Sylvia thought, a touch of fear. "Where did you find that?" she whispered.

"Buried under the Oldest Oak," Dana said in a low voice.

"But how—when—" Bewildered, the businesswoman scanned the room, her two assistants frowning, looking ready to pounce and throw Dana and Sylvia out of the room at a word from their boss. "You two girls—come with me." She stepped over to the side of the room and opened a door. As the two men leaped to follow, she shook her head at them.

"Sylvia, what—" Mrs. Widden put a hand on her shoulder, looking bewildered and very nervous.

"It's okay, Mom," she told her. "Dana and I found something in the woods that belonged to Ms. Maven when she was young. Really, it's okay."

Mrs. Widden stepped back, still looking uncertain, and Sylvia trailed behind Dana into the next room, Margaret Maven's private office. The door closed firmly behind them.

~ Chapter Eleven ~

Margaret Maven silently gestured for Sylvia and Dana to sit. Their feet sank into the plush, moss-green carpeting as they walked across the large room and sat in two blocky-looking, light brown wooden chairs with dark leather seats, set in front of a huge desk made of the same wood. On the wall behind the desk were built-in bookshelves, the lower ones filled with thick, official-looking volumes, the upper ones with framed photographs, many of buildings, a few of people. Next to the chair behind the desk was a standing lamp, the tall wooden base carved, the rounded shade made of blue, white, and green stained glass, the pieces cut in leaf and flower shapes. Everything was very old-fashioned looking, in a simple but elegant way.

When the girls were seated, Margaret Maven went behind the desk and set the geode on top of her desk blotter. She sat down, then reached up and pulled the dangling metal chain of the lamp, which cast an instant soft glow. As the woman sat there staring at the geode, the hardness in her manner fell away. The years, in fact, seemed to fall away, and Sylvia could see traces of the face of the girl they'd seen on their Ethereal dream-journey emerging.

"Have you opened it?" The businesswoman's voice faltered.

Dana and Sylvia shook their heads.

"We thought you should," Dana said.

With hands trembling a little, Margaret reached across the desk, placing both of her palms around the stone. She held it for a moment, then took a deep breath and pulled the halves apart.

When the rock opened, a ripple rolled through the room, as if the air were a pond and the geode had just been tossed into the center. Sylvia could almost feel the force of Margaret's memories surfacing, then pouring out, like a new wellspring opening in a dry place. Onto the desk, a perfect dandelion fell, unwilted, still deep yellow, fresh as if it had been picked in the past hour.

"How on earth—" Margaret Maven started to say in wondering astonishment. But before any more words came out, a wispy yellow funnel rose from the flower, spinning quickly into a sphere, then growing larger, flattening out into a whirling wheel of bright gold. A moment later, an impish, childlike face and glittering topaz eyes met Sylvia's.

"It's the dandelion faery!" Sylvia was delighted. She'd met him last summer, during the drought, the first real faery she'd ever seen.

He dipped and soared around the room, circling the amazed woman's head so fast, he was a blur, making it look like she was wearing a crown.

"'How in the Ether,' you mean," Dana said, grinning.

"I'd forgotten. How could I have forgotten?" Margaret Maven seemed to be asking herself the question. She looked up at the faery and laughed out loud, a sound like rust falling off a musical instrument. Then she looked at Sylvia and Dana. "Friends of Faeries," she said, as if she'd just recognized someone she'd been looking for in a crowd.

Sylvia and Dana sat in silence, watching as Margaret's fingers, shaking a little, crept across the desk to the tiny blue bottle and the good luck rock. She picked them up, and instantly something started happening to the office.

The blue pieces in the stained-glass lamp shade began to glow with the intensity of a low gas flame, and the green pieces began to quiver and push out of the shade, multiplying rapidly. At the same time, the base of the lamp roughened, thickened, and transformed into the slender trunk of a sapling, but quickly growing larger. The huge solid desk and the chairs were shimmering as if the molecules of the wood were coming apart. Everything wavered in front of Sylvia's eyes.

"The carpeting!" Sylvia exclaimed. Beneath their feet, the fibers had softened, grown finer and taller, and a newly mowed lawn smell was wafting up. Without understanding how, she found herself sitting on a patch of grass next to Dana and across from Margaret Maven, who still clutched the blue bottle and the small rock. The two halves of the geode lay on the grass between them. The dandelion child chuckled, flew straight up, and there was no ceiling to stop him. He disappeared into a pale blue sky.

The lamp-tree was massive now, with bits of blue light brightening among a bower of green leaves.

"The Oldest Oak," Dana murmured.

"Are we really here?" Sylvia whispered back.

Before Dana had a chance to give an answer, all the blue lights merged into one, and the light moved slowly down the trunk. At the bottom, a figure wearing a deep blue robe stepped out of the light.

"Mr. MacCooney!" Dana, Sylvia, and Margaret all spoke at the same time.

He walked toward them, holding a book about the size of an encyclopedia, with heavy, blue stone covers, marbled with gold veins. Sylvia instantly recognized it.

"*The Ethereal Blue Book* was at my house," Dana said wonderingly. "How did it—how did you—?"

Mr. MacCooney smiled, but it was a serious smile. "It's time to write the last chapter, now, the final Bardic record of the fate of the Wildbrook Domain and the Fairy Lair." He handed the book to Dana and held up a finger as if telling her to wait, then turned and addressed the speechless businesswoman. "So you've returned, Margaret. Do you recall the last time we met and what you said?"

She looked troubled, but nodded slowly and began to recite:

"*Place of Magic, Faery home,*
Sylph, Salamander, Undine, Gnome,
Use your power to change what's planned
Let the Wildbrook trees all stand.
Special gifts I bring to you.
Grant my wish, if magic's true."

Mr. MacCooney nodded gently, and Sylvia realized those must have been the words she and Dana had missed when Sylvia got lost in the Ether.

"I guess I stopped believing in the magic because my wish didn't work," Margaret said. "My father still cut down a lot of the trees to build the houses on Wildbrook Commons Lane. At first I thought it was because my poem wasn't good enough." She chuckled a little, as if embarrassed. "I wasn't meant to be a Bard. Anyway, after that, I didn't waste thoughts on wishing for things. I just tried to make them happen through my own efforts."

Mr. MacCooney smiled. "Your wish wasn't wasted. It saved all of Wildbrook Woods above the river."

"That wasn't good enough for me back then. Father thought me most ungrateful when he told me he'd changed a part of the plan to make me happy. I didn't speak to him for weeks." She paused, a little sheepishly. "I guess I inherited my stubbornness from him."

"If you felt that way about the woods and the trees, and knew the faeries, how could you grow up to even think about doing what you're going to do?" Sylvia blurted out before she could help it.

Now Margaret looked confused. "I—I don't know. Maybe I grew up to be more like my father than I ever realized." She looked around the glade, which seemed to be becoming more solid and real by the moment.

"May I?" Mr. MacCooney said now. He held out his hand, and she put the tiny blue bottle and the good luck rock in his palm. He reached down and picked up one-half of the geode, turning it upside down on the grass. Then he uncapped the bottle and poured the water over the rock. Instantly it grew larger and larger. More water kept pouring out of the bottle than Sylvia thought it could possibly hold, flowing into a shallow pool around the growing rock.

"The spring! And the boulder! But where's the Ring of Rocks?" Dana looked up at Mr. MacCooney.

His blue eyes twinkled, and he took the good luck stone and skipped it across the water's surface. It swung around the edge like a boomerang with each skip, leaving another rock in place.

Something about the Fairy Lair was different from before. Sylvia couldn't pinpoint exactly what . . . not bigger, but—maybe fuller, somehow? As if crowded with some unseen power that kept gathering.

"Now, Dana," Mr. MacCooney said.

Dana handed *The Ethereal Blue Book* back to him. He opened to the end. The page was blank.

"And for you, Margaret, a decision, which will

write the last page." He set the open book down on top of the boulder, then drew himself up until he seemed taller than Sylvia'd ever seen him before. From a fold in his robe he pulled out an acorn top, cupped it between his thumbs, put it to his lips, and blew into it. A clear, deep whistle, strong as a trumpet note, pierced the air. Putting it away, he spoke loudly enough to rustle the leaves on the trees, which seemed to Sylvia to be getting thicker, bigger, and greener by the minute.

"Ancient Foresters, come you all
At the Oak Master's summoning call."

There was a stirring in the still air in the trees around the perimeter of the glade, and a darkening of deep green shadows, which thickened, then began to move toward the center where they all stood. From the moving shadow, figures began to emerge, men and women, some old, some fairly young, and some whose age Sylvia couldn't begin to guess. All of them wore robes of varying shades of green and brown.

"Look—there's my grandmother!" Dana yanked Sylvia's sleeve and pointed.

Sylvia's jaw dropped. One of the women in the robes did look like Grannie Brennan, only with all her aged wrinkles smoothed out. "Are you sure?"

"Yes, I'm sure. Even if I hadn't seen old pictures of her, I'd be sure," Dana said. "See what she's carrying?"

Sylvia saw—the green glass ball, clear now without a trace of fog in it. She watched as Grannie placed the ball in Mr. MacCooney's outstretched hand.

"By the green glass ball, stay away evil, all!" they said together. The globe began to expand rapidly, the glass thinning, the color lightening until it was barely detectable, like a bubble being blown by a giant, soon encompassing the whole glade, then moving beyond until they couldn't see the edges anymore.

Margaret Maven took a few steps, then slowly turned around, taking it all in. "How could I have forgotten?" She asked herself the question for a second time. "Of course," she murmured, then looked at Dana, Sylvia, and Mr. MacCooney. "Of course." A genuine smile softened her face.

Dana raised her eyebrows questioningly.

"Wildbrook Woods will remain an open space. I'll have the papers drawn up right away."

As soon as she spoke the words aloud, all the invisibly swelling magic burst into the glade at once. The spring bubbled with the clear, sleek forms of Undines splashing. Wispy clouds rolled down from the sky, and from them the graceful air faeries, the Sylphs, began to weave in and out of the treetops. The tiny beginnings of leaves on each branch of each tree spurted with visible growth, forming the pale green faces of the Layshee, the forest guardians. And from every small wildflower, a tiny flower faery flitted out.

In the damp ground around the outside of the new Ring of Rocks, skunk cabbage shoots had pushed up. Now the little round cabbage faeries began to roll out, bouncing happily across the grass. At the same time, a pulse, like a distant, deep drumbeat, began to pound softly. The crevice in the boulder opened, and the tiny guys with tools marched out. Their captain saluted Sylvia with a jaunty grin on his wrinkled little face, then he and his crew swarmed all over the outside of the immense rock and set to work, chiseling away at the boulder.

"What are they doing?" Sylvia said.

"Carving the path to the most Magic Place," Mr. MacCooney said cryptically.

As the gnomes worked away, something else was happening. From all over the glade, orange-red Salamanders were advancing to the edge of the Ring of Rocks. When they'd formed their own ring around it, they began to back away, actually pulling the tiny shoreline away with them, stretching it so the spring began to spread. It spread right beneath their feet, under the gathered group of Ancient Foresters, to the edges of the glade. The water rose over their ankles, then up to their knees.

"It's not wet!" Sylvia said, dipping her hand down into the deepening pool, which was infused with light from the Salamanders and the sun. "It's—what is it?"

"It's magic," Margaret Maven said softly.

It was over their heads now, dense but clear, refreshing, breathable as the cleanest air, and they all, people and elementals, were floating in it. Light in every color of the spectrum was starting to shimmer up the sides, which were growing taller and taller and shaping into walls of light like an enclosed medieval city. The trees disappeared behind the walls, which soon towered high overhead, marked at four corners like the points of a diamond or a compass by four turrets. One for each of the four faery cities, Sylvia knew, Gorias, Murias, Finias, Falias.

Now the gnomes sprang away from the boulder. Or what had been the boulder! Sylvia gasped. The Earth elementals had sculpted the boulder into an enormous rose, its former dull gray color polished to an opalescent sheen. From the center of the blooming stone, the spring now gushed up into a fountain that sprayed down on the pages of *The Ethereal Blue Book.*

A wind swirled around the fountain, through the mist, humming a tune like the sound of a moistened finger circling the rim of a crystal goblet. A most familiar tune to Sylvia, one she'd first heard Mr. MacCooney singing in his garden, the melody that her sister Annie had tried to play on her recorder, summoning the pixies, the music faeries, in the process. Now Mr. MacCooney joined in with the words:

> *"City of East, City of West*
> *City of South, City of North*
> *In the center is the Rose*
> *Where the City of Light shines forth.*
> *Gorias, Murias, day to night*
> *Finias, Falias, point a'right*
> *Sylph and Gnome, Flame and Sprite,*
> *Spiral toward . . ."*

"The City of Light!" Sylvia sang the final words with him. The faery capital, the center toward which all the roads from the four faery cities led, where she and Dana had been once before. They were here!

From each of the four turrets of the elements, a path

was opening, faeries and foresters moving aside, as if to let dignitaries through.

"It's Gneissus, King of the Gnomes," Dana said, nodding toward a craggy-faced, serious-looking man wrapped in a dark gray cloak.

"And Cerundula and Ariella," Sylvia said excitedly. "They're both here, too." The blue-green robes of the Undine queen and the misty silver veils of the Queen of Sylphs flowed behind them as they converged toward the center of the city. "But who's that?"

The fourth figure, a tall man, wore armor that glowed as if permanently burnished by the sun. Smoke trailed behind him, a white puff rising up from each footstep.

"It has to be the Fire King," Dana said.

"Pyrus," Mr. MacCooney told her. "King of the Salamanders, Wildbrook Domain."

Sylvia cast a sidelong glance at Margaret Maven, who seemed stunned with each new thing that occurred, each new elemental presence that appeared. The four domain leaders approached her now, and each bowed to her as if in thanks, then to Sylvia, Dana, and Mr. MacCooney.

"It's time," he said. "To dictate the last chapter of *The Ethereal Blue Book*, the Annals of the Wildbrook

Domain." He looked at Margaret. "Your decision is final?"

"Yes," she said firmly. "It's final. I hereby announce the creation of the Wildbrook Land Trust."

He held his hand up in the air. A wing-shadow passed over, and a long feather floated down, white tinged with blue. Handing it to Dana, he gestured for her to approach the book.

"What do I write?" Sylvia heard Dana's question inside her head, and a rhythm started sloshing. From where, she wasn't sure, but words began to form into phrases, some in her voice, some in Dana's. Dana looked at her and grinned.

"I guess we have a new Bard in the neighborhood," she said, then set to work inscribing the blank page.

"What does the last chapter say?" Margaret Maven asked softly when Dana stepped back, returning the feather to Mr. MacCooney.

"Read it," he told her.

Leaning over the volume, Margaret Maven began to read.

> "*Place of magic, special place*
> *Now official open space*
> *Forever free Wildbrook Domain*

Real—Ethereal will remain.
Both worlds to you we entrust.
Take the measures that you must.
Human friends and Friends of Faeries
Saved, by you, the Faery Lair.'"

As she spoke, her voice resonated through the City of Light. As soon as she finished, *The Ethereal Blue Book* closed, and the walls began to melt into a great, slowly spinning whirlpool of elements. In an instant, it dissolved, leaving them standing in the glade with the Ancient Foresters. All wearing smiles, they began to retreat into the shadows and fade. Sylvia caught Dana's grandmother giving them a quick wave and a wink before she disappeared from view.

Sylvia gave her head a shake as her mind tried to keep up with the transformation.

"Real? Ethereal?" Margaret Maven was murmuring.

"Both," Mr. MacCooney said. He pointed at the boulder, which, though no longer a rose, bore new creases and crevices that suggested it could be, if one could see beneath the surface. He stepped back toward the Oldest Oak and, before Sylvia could blink, winked into a sparkler burst of blue light that flew up into the emerald leaves, blinding her for an instant.

When her eyes focused again, she found herself staring at the lamp shade in Margaret Maven's office. Dana was rubbing her eyes, and Margaret Maven was looking dazed. There was a new wooden plaque hanging on the wall behind her desk, beautifully carved with runes.

> *Margaret Maven of Wildbrook*
> *Friend of Faeries*
> *Friend of Fire, Water, Air*
> *and Earth.*

Startled, Sylvia realized she'd read the runes without any help translating.

She looked at Margaret Maven, who was holding out two more plaques, one to her, one to Dana. "These appear to be for you," she said.

Sylvia took hers and read it.

> *Sylvia Widden*
> *Friend of Faeries*
> *Honorary Citizen of the City of Light.*

Dana's, inscribed with her name, said the same.

"Well, that was quite a meeting," Dana said, shaking her head a little.

"Oh my goodness! The meeting—all those people in

the conference room!" Ms. Maven's gaze shot to the office door. "How long have we kept them waiting?" She held her wrist up and looked at her watch, then frowned, tapping it.

"What time is it?" Sylvia asked.

The businesswoman looked at Sylvia, then Dana, then smiled.

"It's stopped—my watch. And it's time to stop the wrong kind of progress—to set things straight about the fate of Wildbrook Domain." She stood, catching sight of the new plaque as she did. Her smile widened, and she took a step toward the door, then stopped and gestured for Sylvia and Dana to go first. "After you, my friends."

Sometimes one day can change a life forever

AMERICAN *Diaries*

Different girls,
living in different periods of America's past
reveal their hearts' secrets in the pages
of their diaries. Each one faces a challenge
that will change her life forever.
Don't miss any of their stories: